Marrying HIS MAJESTY

She'll be his bride—by royal decree!

**The crowns of the Diamond Isles
are about to return to their rightful heirs:
three gorgeous Mediterranean princes.
But their road to royal matrimony is
lined with secrets, lies and forbidden love....**

In September
Claimed: Secret Royal Son
A year ago Lily became accidentally pregnant
with Prince Alexandros's baby. Now Alex wants to
claim his secret royal son—and a convenient wife!

Last month
Betrothed: To the People's Prince
Nikos is the people's prince, but the crown of Argyros
belongs to the reluctant Princess Athena—
the woman he was forbidden to marry.
Can Nikos finally persuade her to come home?

This month
Crowned: The Palace Nanny
For Elsa, nanny to the nine-year-old heiress
to the throne of Khryseis, Zoe, there's more in store
than going to the ball. Can this Cinderella
win the heart of the new prince regent?

*Join Marion Lennox on the Diamond Isles
for three resplendent royal romances!*

MARION LENNOX

Crowned: The Palace Nanny

Marrying
HIS MAJESTY

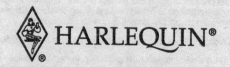

HARLEQUIN®

TORONTO • NEW YORK • LONDON
AMSTERDAM • PARIS • SYDNEY • HAMBURG
STOCKHOLM • ATHENS • TOKYO • MILAN • MADRID
PRAGUE • WARSAW • BUDAPEST • AUCKLAND

Recycling programs
for this product may
not exist in your area.

ISBN-13: 978-0-373-17620-5

CROWNED: THE PALACE NANNY

First North American Publication 2009.

Copyright © 2009 by Marion Lennox.

www.eHarlequin.com

Printed in U.S.A.

Marion Lennox is a country girl, born on an Australian dairy farm. She moved on—mostly because the cows just weren't interested in her stories! Married to a "very special doctor," Marion writes for the Harlequin® Romance line. (She used a different name for a while—if you're looking for her past Harlequin Romance novels, search for author Trisha David, as well.) She's now had more than seventy-five romance novels accepted for publication.

In her non-writing life Marion cares for kids, cats, dogs, chickens and goldfish. She travels, and she fights her rampant garden (she's losing) and her house dust (she's lost).

Having spun in circles for the first part of her life, she's now stepped back from her "other" career, which was teaching statistics at her local university. Finally she's reprioritized her life, figured out what's important and discovered the joys of deep baths, romance and chocolate. Preferably all at the same time!

This season Harlequin® Romance brings you

Christmas Treats

For an extra-special treat this Christmas
don't look under the Christmas tree or in
your stocking—pick up one of your favorite
Harlequin Romance novels, curl up and relax!

From presents to proposals, mistletoe to marriage,
we promise to deliver seasonal warmth, wonder
and of course the unbeatable rush of romance!

*And look out for Christmas surprises
this month in Harlequin Romance!*

CHAPTER ONE

DR ELSA LANGHAM disappeared after a car accident four years ago. Mrs Elsa Murdoch took her place.

The invitation had been sitting on the table all day, a taunting reminder of her past.

> The International Coral Society invites Dr Elsa Langham, foremost authority on Coral: Alcyonacea, to submit a paper at this year's symposium in Hawaii.

The ICS hadn't kept up with her change in direction. Eight-year-old Zoe was asleep in the next room, totally dependent on her, and Dr Elsa Langham was no longer an acclaimed authority on anything.

She read the invitation one last time, sighed and finally dumped it in the bin.

'I don't know why they're still sending me invitations,' she told the skinny black cat slinking out from under her chair. 'I'm Mrs Elsa Murdoch, a mother to Zoe, an occasional student of starfish to keep my scientific hand in, and my cats need feeding.'

She rose and took a bowl of cat food to the back garden. The little cat followed, deeply suspicious but seduced by the smell of supper.

Four more cats were waiting. Elsa explained the terms of their tenancy as she did every night, fed them, then ignored five feline glares as she locked them up for the night. They knew the deal, but they didn't have to like it.

'At least you guys go free every morning,' she told them. 'You can do what you want during the day.'

And so could she, she told herself. She could take Zoe to the beach. She could study starfish. She could be Mrs Elsa Murdoch.

Until a miracle happens, she thought to herself, pausing to look up at the night sky. Not that I need a miracle. I really love Zoe, I don't mind starfish and I'm incredibly lucky to be alive. It's just…I wouldn't mind a bit of magic. Like a rainbow of coral to appear in our cove. Or Prince Charming to wave his wand and take away my debts and Zoe's scars.

Enough. The cats weren't interested in wishes, and neither was anyone else. She smiled ruefully into the night, turned her back on her disgruntled cats and went inside. She needed to fix a blocked sink.

Where was Prince Charming when you needed him?

The little boy would live.

Prince Stefanos Antoniadis—Dr Steve to his patients— walked out of Theatre savouring a combination of triumph and exhaustion. He'd won.

The boy's mother—a worn-looking woman with no English, but with a smile wide enough to cut through any language barrier—hugged him and cried, and Stefanos hugged her back and felt his exhaustion disappear.

He felt fantastic.

He walked into the scrub room, sorely tempted to punch the air in triumph—and then stopped dead.

This wasn't fantastic. This was trouble.

Two months ago, King Giorgos of the Diamond Isles had died without an heir. Next in line to the throne of the Mediterranean island of Khryseis was Stefanos's cousin, Christos. The only problem was, no one could find Christos. Worse, if Christos couldn't be found, the throne belonged to Stefanos—who wanted the crown like a hole in the head.

In desperation he'd employed a friend who moved in diplomatic circles and whose discretion he trusted absolutely to search internationally for Christos. That his friend was here to tell him the news in person meant there must be a major problem.

'They told me you've been opening a kid's skull, chopping bits out and sticking it back together,' his friend said with easy good humour. 'How hard's that? *Seven hours…*'

'I get paid by the hour,' Stefanos said, grasping his friend's hand. But he couldn't make himself smile. 'What news?'

'From your point of view?' As an investigator this man was the best, and he knew the issues involved. 'You're not Crown Prince of Khryseis.'

'Not!' He closed his eyes. The relief was almost overwhelming.

It hadn't always been like this. As a boy, Stefanos had even dreamed of inheriting the throne that his almost pathologically shy cousin swore he didn't want.

But that was in the past. King Giorgos was bound to have sons, and if not… Christos would just have to wear it. Almost twenty years ago, Stefanos had moved to the States to pursue a medical career. His dream since then had been to perfect and teach surgical techniques, so wounds such as the ones he'd treated today could be repaired in hospitals less specialised than this one, anywhere in the world. 'So you've finally found Christos?' he asked, feeling the weight of the world lift from his shoulders.

'Sort of,' his friend said, but there was something in his face which made Stefanos's jubilation fade. His expression said that whatever was coming wasn't good.

'Christos is dead, Steve,' the man said gently. 'In a car accident in Australia, four years ago. That's why you haven't been able to find him.'

'Dead.' He stared at his friend in horror. 'Christos? My cousin. Why? How?'

'You know he left the island soon after you? Apparently he

and his mother emigrated to Australia. Neither of them kept in touch. It seems his mother held his funeral with no fuss, and contacted no one back on Khryseis. Three months after he died, so did she.'

'Dear God.'

'It's the worst of news,' his friend said. He hesitated. 'But there's more.'

Stefanos knew it. He was replaying their conversation in his head. His friend's first words had been, 'You're not Crown Prince of Khryseis.'

Christos had been first in line to the throne, followed by Stefanos. But Christos was dead. Therefore it had to be Stefanos. Unless…

'There's a child,' his friend told him.

'A child,' he said numbly.

'A little girl. Christos married, but his wife was killed in the same accident. Their child survived. She was four when her parents were killed. She's now eight.'

Stefanos didn't respond. He was staring at his friend, but he was seeing nothing.

He was working on groundbreaking surgical techniques. His work here was vital.

A child.

'Her name's Zoe,' his friend said. 'She's still living in Australia with a woman called Mrs Elsa Murdoch, who seems to be employed as her nanny. But, Steve…'

'Yes?' But he already knew what was coming.

'Christos's death means the child takes the Crown,' he said gently. 'Zoe's now the Crown Princess of Khryseis. That means you're Prince Regent.'

Stefanos still didn't answer. There was a chasm opening before him—a gaping void where his career used to be. He could only listen while his friend told him what he'd learned.

'I've done some preliminary checks. From what I gather of the island's constitution, you'll be in charge until Zoe's twenty-five. The island's rule, and the consequent care of your cousin as Crown Princess, lies squarely on your shoulders. Now…do you want me to find an address for this woman called Elsa?'

CHAPTER TWO

ROYALTY was standing on Elsa's beach.

Sunlight was shimmering from the surface of a turquoise sea. The tide was at its lowest for months. Their beach was a mass of rock pools and there were specimens everywhere.

They'd swum far out to the buoy marking the end of shallow water and a pod of dolphins had nosed in to check them out. They'd dived for starfish. They'd floated lazily in the shallows; floating eased the nagging ache in Elsa's hip as nothing else could. Finally they'd made each other crowns out of seaweed pods, and now Queen Elsa and her consort, Princess Zoe, were marching back to the house for lunch and a nap.

To find royalty waiting for them. Royalty without seaweed.

For a moment Elsa thought she'd been out in the sun too long. The man was dressed like a prince from one of Zoe's picture books. His uniform was black as night, tailored to perfection. His slick-fitting suit was adorned with crimson epaulettes, tassels, braid and medals. His jacket and the top collar of his shirt were unbuttoned, but for some reason that made him look even more princely.

A prince trying to look casual?

Uh-oh. Her hand flew to her seaweed crown and she tugged it off as icy tendrils of fear crept round her heart.

Royalty was fantasy. Not real. Zoe's father had always been afraid of it, but his stories had seemed so far-fetched that Elsa had deemed them ludicrous.

'Look,' Zoe said, puzzled, and the eight-year-old's hand clutched hers. Zoe had only been four when her parents died, but maybe she remembered enough of her father's paranoia to worry.

Or maybe the sight of someone dressed as a prince on a Queensland beach was enough to worry anyone.

'I can see him,' Elsa said. 'Wow. Do you think he's escaped from your *Sleeping Beauty* book?'

'He's gorgeous,' Zoe said, relaxing a little as Elsa deliberately made light of it.

'He must be hot,' Elsa said cautiously.

'Do you think he came in a carriage like in *Cinderella*?'

'If he did, I hope it has air-conditioning,' Elsa retorted and Zoe giggled.

Good. Great. Zoe giggling was far more important than any prince watching them from the sand dunes.

She would not let anything interfere with that giggle.

'Maybe he's looking for us,' Zoe said, worry returning. 'Maybe he's from Khryseis.'

'Maybe he is.' Neither of them had ever been to Khryseis, but the fabulous Mediterranean island was part of Zoe's heritage—home to the father who'd been killed when she was four. According to the Internet, Khryseis was an island paradise in the Mediterranean, ruled up until now by a King who was as corrupt as he was vindictive. Zoe's father, Christos, had spoken occasionally of the old King's malice. Now those stories came flooding back, and Elsa's fears increased accordingly.

The man—the prince?—was walking down the sandy track towards them, tall, tanned and drop-dead gorgeous. Elsa stopped and put down her pail. She held Zoe's hand tighter.

A lesser mortal might look ridiculous in this situation but, despite his uniform, this man looked to be in charge of his world. Strongly built, aquiline features, dark hooded eyes. Cool, authoritative and calm.

And then he smiled. The combination of uniform, body and smile was enough to knock a girl's socks off. If she had any socks that was, she thought, humour reasserting itself as she decided it was ridiculous to be afraid. She wiggled her toes deep into the sand, feeling the need to ground herself.

Oh, but that smile…

Down, she told herself fiercely. Hormonal response was exactly what wasn't wanted right now. Act cool.

She met the man's gaze and deliberately made herself match his smile. Or almost match it. Her smile was carefully that of someone passing a stranger. His smile, on the other hand, was friendly. His gaze dropped to Zoe—and his smile died. That always happened. No one could stop that initial reaction.

Instinctively Elsa tugged Zoe closer but Zoe was already there. They braced together, waiting for the usual response. Try as she might, she couldn't protect Zoe from strangers. Her own scars were more easily hidden, but Zoe's were still all too obvious.

But this wasn't a normal response. 'Zoe,' the man said softly, on a long drawn-out note of discovery. And pleasure. 'You surely must be Zoe. You look just like your father.'

Neither of them knew what to say to that. They stood in the brilliant sunlight while Elsa tried to think straight.

She felt foolish, and that was dumb. She was wearing shorts and an old shirt, and she'd swum in what she was wearing. Her sun-bleached hair had been tied in a ponytail this morning, but her curls had escaped while she swam. She was coated in sand and salt, and her nose was starting to peel.

Ditto for Zoe.

They were at the beach in Australia. They were appropriately dressed, she thought, struggling for defiance. Whereas this man…

'I'm sorry I'm in uniform,' he said, as if guessing her thoughts. 'I know it looks crazy, but I've pulled in some favours trying to find you. Those favours had to be repaid in the form of attending a civic reception as soon as I landed. I left as soon as I could, but the media's staked out my hotel. If

I'd stopped to change they might well have followed me here. I don't want Zoe to be inundated by the press yet.'

Whoa. There was way too much in that last statement to take in. First of all… Was he really royal? What was she supposed to do? Bow?

Not on your life.

'So…who are you?' she managed, and Zoe said nothing.

'I'm Stefanos. Prince Regent of Khryseis. Zoe, your grandfather and my grandfather were brothers. Your father and I were cousins. I guess that makes us cousins of sorts too.'

Cousins. That was almost enough to make her knees give way. Zoe had relations?

This man's voice had the resonance of a Greek accent, not strong but unmistakable. That wasn't enough to confirm anything.

'Christos didn't have any cousins,' she said, which was maybe dumb—what would she know? 'Or…he always said there was no one. So did his mother.'

'And I didn't know they'd died,' he said gently. 'Zoe, I'm so sorry. I knew your father and I knew your grandmother, and I loved them both. I'm very sorry I didn't keep in touch. I'm so sorry I wasn't here when you so obviously needed me.'

Elsa was starting to shake. She so didn't want to be shaking when Zoe was holding her hand, but it was happening regardless.

She was all Zoe had. And—she might as well admit it— for the last four years Zoe was all she'd had.

'You can't have her.' It was said before she had a chance to think, before her head even engaged. It was pure panic and it was infectious. Zoe froze.

'I'm not going with you,' she whispered, and then her voice rose in panic to match Elsa's. 'I'm not, I'm not.' And she buried her face against Elsa and sobbed her terror. Elsa swung her up into her arms and held. The little girl was clutching her as if she were drowning.

And Stefanos…or whoever he was…was staring at them

both in bemusement. She looked at him over Zoe's head and found his expression was almost quizzical.

'Good one,' he said dryly. 'You don't think you might be overreacting just a little?'

She probably was, she conceded, hugging Zoe tighter, but there was no room for humour here.

'You think we might be a bit over the top?' she managed. 'Prince Charming on a Queensland beach.' She looked past him and saw a limousine—a Bentley, no less, with a chauffeur to boot. Overreaction? She didn't think so. 'You're frightening Zoe. You're frightening me.'

'I didn't come to frighten you.'

'So why did you come?' She heard herself then, realising she was sounding hysterical. She knew Zoe's father had come from Khryseis. She knew he'd been part of the royal family. What could be more natural than a distant relative, here on official business, dropping in to see Zoe?

But then there was his statement… *I've pulled in some favours trying to find you.* He'd deliberately come searching for Zoe.

Prince Regent… That made him Prince in charge while someone was incapacitated. The old King?

Or when someone was a child.

No.

'Zoe, hush,' she said, catching her breath, deciding someone had to be mature and it might as well be her. 'I was silly to panic. Stefanos isn't here to take you away.' She glared over Zoe's head, as much to tell him, *Don't you dare say anything different.* 'He comes from the island where your papa grew up. I'm sorry I reacted like I did. I was very rude and very silly. I think it's time to dry our eyes and meet him properly.'

Zoe hiccuped on a sob, but there'd been worse things than this to frighten Zoe in her short life, and she was one brave little girl. She sniffed and wiped her eyes with the back of her hand and turned within Elsa's arms to face him.

She was a whippet of a child, far too thin, and far too small.

The endless operations had taken their toll. It was taking time and painstaking rehabilitation to build her up to anywhere near normal.

'Maybe we both should say sorry and a proper hello,' Elsa said ruefully, and Zoe swallowed manfully and put a thin hand out in greeting. Clinging to Elsa with the other.

'Hello,' she whispered.

'Hello,' Stefanos said and took her hand with all the courtesy of one royal official meeting another. 'I'm very pleased to meet you, Zoe. I've come halfway round the world to meet you.'

And then he turned his attention to Elsa. 'And you must be Mrs Murdoch.'

'She's Elsa,' Zoe corrected him.

'Elsa, then, if that's okay with Elsa,' Stefanos said, meeting her gaze steadily. She had no hand free left to shake and she was glad of it. This man was unsettling enough without touch.

So... She didn't know where to go from here. Did you invite a prince home for a cup of tea? Or for a twelve course luncheon?

'You live here?' he asked, his tone still gentle. There was only one place in sight. Her bungalow—a tired, rundown shack. 'Is this place yours?'

'Yes.'

'Can I come in and talk to you?'

'Your chauffeur...'

'Would it be too much trouble to ask if you could ring for a taxi to take me back into town when we've spoken? I don't like to keep my chauffeur waiting.'

'There's no taxi service out here.'

'Oh.'

Now what? What was a woman to say when a prince didn't want to keep his chauffeur waiting? She needed an instruction manual. Maybe she was still verging on the hysterical.

She gave herself a swift mental shake. 'I'm sorry. A taxi won't come out here but we have a car. It'll only take us fifteen minutes to run you back into town. I'm not normally so…so inhospitable. It's the uniform.'

'I expect it might be,' he said and smiled, and there it was again, that smile—a girl could die and go to heaven in that smile. 'I don't want to put you to trouble.'

'If you can cope with a simple sandwich, you're welcome to lunch,' she managed. 'And…of course we'll drive you into town. After all, you're Christos's cousin.'

'So I can't be all bad?' It was a teasing question and she flushed.

'I loved Christos,' she said, almost defensively. 'And I loved Amy. Zoe's mama and papa were my closest friends.' She managed a shaky smile. 'For their sake…you're welcome.'

The house was saggy and battered and desperately in need of a paint. A couple of weatherboards had crumbled under the front window and a piece of plywood had been tacked in place to fill the gap. The whole place looked as if it could blow over in the next breeze. Only the garden, fabulous and overgrown, looked as if it was holding the place together.

Stefanos hardly noticed the garden. All he noticed was the woman in front of him.

She was…stunning. Stunning in every sense of the word, he thought. Natural, graceful, free.

Free was maybe a dumb adjective but it was the thought that came to mind. She was wearing nothing but shorts and a faded white blouse, its top three buttons undone so he had a glimpse of beautiful cleavage. Her long slim legs seemed to go on for ever, finally ending in bare feet, tanned and sand coated. This woman lived in bare feet, he thought, and a shiver went through him that he couldn't identify. Was it weird to think bare sandy toes were incredibly sexy? If it was, then count him weird.

But it wasn't just her toes. It wasn't just her body.

Her face was tanned, with wide intelligent eyes, a smattering of freckles and a full generous mouth with a lovely smile.

Breathtakingly lovely. Her honey-blonde hair was sun-kissed, bleached to almost translucence by the sun. There was no way those streaks were artificial, for there was nothing artificial about this woman. She wore not a hint of make-up, except the remains of a smear of white suncream over her nose, and her riot of damp, salt-and-sand-laden curls looked as if they hadn't seen a comb for a week.

Quite simply, he'd never seen a woman so beautiful.

'Are you coming in?' Elsa was standing on the veranda, looking at him with the beginnings of amusement. Probably because he was standing with his mouth open.

'Is this a holiday shack?' he managed, forcing his focus to the house—though it was almost impossible to force his focus anywhere but her. The information he'd been given said she lived here. Surely not.

'No,' she said shortly, amusement fading. 'It's our home. I promise it's clean enough inside so you won't get your uniform dirty.'

'I didn't mean…'

'No.' She relented and forced another of her lovely smiles. 'I know you didn't. I'm sorry.'

He came up the veranda steps. Zoe had already disappeared inside, and he heard the sound of running water.

'Zoe gets first turn at the shower while I make lunch,' Elsa explained. 'Then she sets the table while I shower.'

It was said almost defiantly. Like—don't mess with the order of things. She was afraid, he thought.

But… This woman was Zoe's nanny. She was being paid out of Zoe's estate. He'd worried when he'd read that—a stranger making money out of a child.

Now he wasn't so sure. This wasn't a normal nanny-child relationship. Even after knowing them only five minutes, he knew it.

And the fear? She'd be wanting reassurance that he wouldn't take Zoe away. He couldn't give it. He watched her face and he knew his silence was being assessed for what it was.

Why hadn't he found more out about her? His information was that Zoe's parents had died in a car crash four years ago. Since then Zoe had been living with a woman who was being paid out of her parents' estate—an estate consisting mostly of Christos's life insurance.

That information had him hoping things could be handled simply. He could take Zoe back to Khryseis and employ a lovely, warm nanny over there to care for her. Maybe this could even be seen as a rescue mission.

This woman, sunburned, freckled and barefoot, standing with her arms folded across her breasts in a stance of pure defence, said it wasn't simple at all. Mrs Elsa Murdoch was not your normal nanny.

And… Christos and Amy had been her best friends?

'I'm not here to harm Zoe,' he said mildly.

'No.' That was a dumb statement, he conceded. As if she was expecting him to beat the child.

'I just want what's best for her.'

'Good,' she said brusquely. 'You might be able to help me. There are a couple of things I could use some advice over.'

That wasn't what he meant. They both knew it.

'Did you know Zoe's the new Crown Princess of Khryseis?' he asked, and she froze.

'The what?'

'The Crown Princess of Khryseis.'

'I heard you. I don't know what you mean.'

'I think you do,' he said softly. 'Your face when I said it…'

'Doesn't mean a thing,' she whispered. 'I'm tired, confused and hungry, and your uniform is doing my head in. Come in and sit down while I make lunch and take a shower. But if you say one word—one word—of this Crown Princess thing to Zoe before we've discussed it fully, you'll be off my property so fast you'll leave your gold tassels behind. Got it?'

'Um…got it,' he said.

'Right,' she said and turned and marched inside, leaving him to follow if he felt like it. Or go away if he felt like it.

Her body language said the second option was the one she favoured.

The moment he got inside he took his jacket off. He pulled off his tie, undid the next two buttons of his shirt and rolled up his sleeves.

It was a casual gesture of making himself at home and it rendered her almost speechless.

Outside he'd seemed large. Inside, tossing his jacket on the settee, rolling up his sleeves, taking a slow visual sweep of her kitchen-living room, he seemed much larger. It was as if he was filling the room, the space not taken up with his sheer physical size overwhelmed by his sheer masculinity.

He was six one or six two, she thought. Not huge. Just…male. And more good-looking than was proper. And way too sexy.

Sexy. Where had that word come from? She shoved it away in near panic.

'This is great,' he said, and she fought for composure and tried to see the house as he saw it.

It was tumbledown. Of course it was. There was no way she could afford to fix the big things. One day in the not too distant future Zoe might be able to go to school and she could take a proper job again and earn some money. But meanwhile they made do.

'Where did you get this stuff?' he asked, gesturing to the room in general. 'It's amazing.'

'Most of it we found or we made.'

He gazed around at the eclectic mix of brightly coloured cushions and faded crimson curtains, the colourful knotted rugs on the floor, lobster pots hanging from the ceiling with shells threaded through to make them look like proper decorations, a fishing net strung across the length of one wall, filled with old buoys and huge seashells. There were worn pottery jugs filled with flowers from the garden; bird of paradise plants, crimson and deep green.

'You found all this?' he demanded.

'I used to have an apartment at the university,' she told him. 'Small. My parents left me this place and I came here at weekends. I'm a marine biologist and we…I used the cottage as an occasional base for research. Zoe's parents were what you might call itinerant. They had a camper van and most of what they owned was destroyed in the accident. So Zoe and I scrounged what we could find, we made a bit and we filled the rest by beachcombing.' She met his gaze full on, defying him to deny her next assertion. 'Zoe and I are the best beach-combers in the world.'

'I can see you are,' he said. He paused. 'You're a marine biologist?'

'Yes.' She faltered and tried for a recovery. 'Very part-time until Zoe goes to school.'

'Zoe doesn't go to school?'

'I home-school her here at the moment.'

'So meanwhile you're living off Christos's life insurance.'

She'd opened the refrigerator and was lifting out salad ingredients. She froze.

She didn't turn around. She couldn't. If she had he might have got lettuce square in the middle of his face. What was he suggesting?

'That's right,' she said stiffly. 'I'm ripping Zoe off for every cent I can get.'

'I didn't mean…'

'I'm very sure you did mean.' Finally she turned, carefully placing the lettuce out of throwing range. 'What is it you want of us, Mr Whoever-The-Hell-You-Are, because there's no way I'm calling you Prince. I don't know why you're here but don't you dare imply I'm acting dishonestly. Don't you dare.'

'I already did,' he said, holding his hands up as if in sur-render. 'I'm sorry.'

'So am I.'

The door swung open. Zoe appeared, looking wary. The

little girl was in clean T-shirt and shorts. Her hair was a tangle of dark, wet curls. She was far too thin, Elsa thought, trying to see her dispassionately through Stefanos's eyes.

She was so scarred. The burns had been to almost fifty per cent of her body, and twenty per cent of those had been full thickness. She'd had graft after graft. Thankfully her face was almost untouched but her skinny little legs looked almost like patchwork. Her left arm still needed work—her left hand was missing its little finger—and there was deep scarring under her chin.

She'd protect this child with her life, she thought, but protection could only go so far. This man was part of Zoe's real family. She had to back off a little.

'Okay, it's my turn for the shower, poppet,' she said, trying to make her voice normal.

'You sounded angry,' she said, doubtful.

'I'm crabby 'cos I'm hungry.' She tugged Zoe to her in a swift hug. 'I'll have a shower in world record time. Can you set the table and talk to…Stefanos. He's your papa's cousin. He knows all about Khryseis. Maybe he could show you exactly where he lives on the Internet. We have pictures of Khryseis bookmarked.'

And, with a final warning glance at Stefanos, she whisked herself away. She didn't want to leave at all. She wanted to bring Zoe into the bathroom with her. She wanted to defend her with everything she had.

Zoe, Crown Princess?

Zoe had far too much to deal with already. If Stefanos wanted to take on part of Zoe's life, then he had to contend with her. Zoe's life was her life. She'd sworn that to Zoe's mother, and she wasn't backing down on it now.

She couldn't. She was so afraid…

CHAPTER THREE

ZOE set the table while he watched her. The little girl was watching him out of the corner of her eye, not meeting his gaze directly. Table done, she turned to a corner desk holding a computer. The machine looked like something out of the Dark Ages, big, cumbersome and ugly. She checked the Internet, waiting until the Khryseis information downloaded—seemingly by slow-boat from China.

But finally the websites in Khryseis were on the screen. By the look of the bookmarks, she and Elsa spent a lot of time browsing them.

He tentatively showed her where he lived on the island— or where he'd lived as a child. She reacted with silent politeness.

He checked the other bookmarks for the island. They were marine sites, he saw. Research articles about the island.

Worth noting.

'So you and Elsa spend a lot of time studying…fish?' he ventured and got a scornful look for his pains.

'Echinoderms.'

Right. Good. What the hell were echinoderms?

And then Elsa was back. Same uniform as before—shorts and faded shirt. She was tugging her curls back into a ponytail. Still she wore no make-up, and without the suncream her freckles were more pronounced. Her nose was peeling and her feet were still bare.

She walked with a slight limp, he noted, but it was very slight. A twisted ankle, maybe? But that was a side issue. He wasn't about to focus on an ankle when he was looking at the whole package.

She was so different from the women in the circles he moved in that her appearance left him stunned. Awed, even.

He'd implied she was dishonest. There was nothing in this place, in her dress, in anything in this house, that said she was taking advantage of Zoe. His investigator had shown him Christos's financial affairs. If they were both living totally on Christos's life insurance...

'How much outside work do you do?' he said, carefully neutral, and Elsa pulled up short.

'You mean how much of my obviously fabulous riches are derived from honest toil and how much by stealing from orphans?'

He had to smile. And, to his relief, she returned a wry smile herself, as if she was ordering herself to relax.

'I'm not accusing you in any sense of the word,' he assured her. 'What's in front of my eyes is Zoe, in need of your care, and you, providing that care. Christos's life insurance wouldn't come close to paying for your combined expenses.'

'You don't know the half of it.'

'So tell me.'

She shook her head. 'I'm sorry, but Christos never spoke of you, as a cousin or as a friend. As far as I know, neither Christos nor his mother ever wanted to have anything to do with anyone from Khryseis. How can my finances have anything to do with you?'

'I do want to help.'

'Is that right?' she said neutrally. She shook her head. 'I'm sorry. Look, can we eat? I can't think while I'm hungry and after a morning on the beach I could eat a horse.'

She almost did. There was cold meat and salad, and freshly baked bread which she tipped from an ancient bread-maker. She cut doorstop slices of bread and made sandwiches. She poured tumblers of home-made lemonade, sat herself down, checked Zoe had what she needed—the sandwich she'd made for Zoe was much smaller, almost delicate in comparison to the ones she'd made for herself and for him—and then proceeded to eat.

She ate two doorstop sandwiches and drank three tumblers of lemonade, while Zoe ate half a sandwich and Elsa prodded her to eat more.

'Those legs are never going to get strong if they're hollow,' she teased, and Zoe gave her a shy smile, threw Stefanos a scared glance and nibbled a bit more.

She was trying to eat. He could see that. Was his presence scaring her?

The idea of frightening this child was appalling. The whole situation was appalling. He was starting to have serious qualms about whether his idea of Zoe's future was possible.

Except it must be. He had to get this child back to Khryseis. Oh, but her little body…

It didn't take his medical qualifications to realise how badly this child was damaged. The report he'd read had told him that four years ago Christos, his wife and their four-year-old daughter had been involved in a major car accident. Christos had died instantly. Amy, his wife, had died almost two weeks later and Zoe, their child, had been orphaned. No details.

There was a story behind every story, he thought, and suddenly he had a flash of what must have happened. A camper van crashing. A fire. A death, a woman so badly burned she died two weeks later, and a child. A child burned like her mother.

He knew enough about burns to understand you didn't get these type of scars without months—years—of medical treatment. Without considerable pain.

He'd arrived here thinking he had an orphaned eight-year-old on his hands. On *his* hands. She'd seemed like one more responsibility to add to his list. Her nanny was listed as one Mrs Elsa Murdoch. He'd had visions of a matronly employee, taking care of a school-aged child in return for cash.

His preconceptions had been so far from the mark that he felt dizzy.

Despite the man-sized sandwich on his plate, he wasn't eating. The official reception had been mid-morning, there'd been canapés, and he'd been watched to see which ones he ate, which chef he'd offend. So he'd eaten far more than he wanted. Elsa's doorstop sandwich was good, but he felt free to leave the second half uneaten. He had a feeling Elsa wasn't a woman who was precious about her cooking.

Actually…was this cooking? He stared down at his sandwich and thought of the delicacies he'd been offered since he'd taken over the throne—and he grinned.

'So what's funny?' Elsa demanded, and he looked up and found she was watching him. Once more she was wearing her assessing expression. He found it penetrating…and disturbing. He didn't like to be read, but he had a feeling that in Elsa Murdoch he'd found someone who could do just that.

'I've had an overload of royal food,' he told her. 'This is great.'

'So you wouldn't be eating…why?'

'I'm full of canapés.'

'I can see that about you,' she said. 'A canapé snacker. Can I have your sandwich, then?'

He handed it over and watched in astonishment as she ate. Where was she putting it? There wasn't an ounce of spare flesh on her. She looked…just about perfect.

Where had that description come from? He thought of the glamorous women he'd had in his life, how appalled they'd be if they could hear the *perfect* adjective applied to this woman, and once more he couldn't help smiling.

'Yep, we're a world away from your world,' she said brusquely.

What the…? 'Will you stop that?'

'What?' she asked, all innocence.

'Mind reading.'

'Not if it works. It's fun.' She rose and started clearing dishes. He noted the limp again but, almost as he noted it, it ceased. Zoe was visibly wilting. 'Zoe, poppet, you go take a nap. Unless…' She paused. 'Unless Stefanos wants us to drive him into town now.'

'I need to talk to you,' he said.

'There you go,' she said equably. 'I mind read that too. So, Zoe, pop into bed and we'll take Stefanos home when you wake up.'

'You won't get angry again?' Zoe asked her, casting an anxious look across at him.

And he got that too. This child's mental state was fragile. She did not need angry voices. She did not need anyone arguing about her future.

This place was perfect for an injured child to heal, he thought. A tropical paradise.

He had another paradise for her, though. He watched with concern as Elsa kissed her soundly, promised her no anger and sent her off to bed.

There was no choice. He just had to make this…nanny… accept it.

She washed.

He wiped.

She protested, but he was on the back foot already—the idea of watching while she worked would make the chasm deeper.

They didn't speak. Maybe the idea of having a prince doing her wiping was intimidating, he thought wryly, and here it was again. Her response before he could voice his thought.

'An apron beats tassels for this job any day. I need a camera,' she said, handing him a sudsy breadboard to wipe. 'No one will believe this.'

'Aren't you supposed to rinse off the suds?'

'You're criticising my washing? I'm more than happy to let you do both.'

'I'm more than happy to do both.'

She paused. She set down her dishcloth and turned to face him, wiping her sudsy hands on the sides of her shorts.

She looked anxious again. And territorial.

And really, really cute.

'Why the limp?' he asked and she glanced at him as if he was intruding where he wasn't wanted.

'It's hardly a limp. I'm fine. Next question?'

'Where's Mr Murdoch?' he asked, and her face grew another emotion.

'What?' she said dangerously.

Uh-oh. But he couldn't take the question back. It hung between them, waiting for an answer.

'My researchers said Zoe's nanny was a Mrs Elsa Murdoch.'

'Ms,' she said and glared.

'So never a Mrs?'

'What's that to do with the price of eggs?'

'It's merely a polite question.'

'Polite. Okay.' She even managed a…polite…smile. 'So where's your Princess?'

'Sorry?'

'I'm Mrs so there has to be a Mr. I believe I'm simply reversing your question. Is there a matching Princess?'

'Why would you want to know that?'

'Exactly,' she said, and smiled—a smile that confounded him as she turned back to her washing. Only there was nothing left to wash. She let the water out and wiped the sink with care. She waited for him to dry the last glass, then wiped his part of the sink as well, as if it was vital that not a speck of anything remained.

This woman confounded him—but he had to focus on their future. He must.

'Zoe's needed back on Khryseis,' he said, and Elsa's hand stilled mid-wipe. She couldn't disguise the fear sweeping over her face.

'She stays here.'

'I believe I'm her nearest living relative,' he said mildly. 'As such I can challenge your guardianship.'

She didn't move. Her hand seemed suddenly to be locked on the sink. She was staring downward as if there was something riveting in its depths.

'Oh…' He couldn't mistake the distress on her face. 'No!'

But it had to be said. Like it or not, the stakes were too high to allow emotion to hold sway.

'I'm her cousin,' he said, gently but as firm as he needed to be. 'It's obvious you're struggling to care for her. I can…'

'You can't.' She whirled to face him at that. Her voice was low enough not to disturb Zoe, but loud enough to make him feel her fury. And her fear. 'She's been with me for four years. I'm her godmother and her guardian. Her mother was my best friend and I promised Amy I'd care for her. Her father was a colleague and I loved him too. You…did you know any of them?'

'I knew Christos.'

'Yeah, close family,' she mocked. 'He never mentioned you. Not once. He said royalty on Khryseis was a shambles, the King was concerned only with himself, the King controlled all three of the Diamond Isles and the original royal families of each island were helpless. Christos was frightened of the royal family. He came here to escape what he saw as persecution. He hated them.'

Okay, he thought. Stick to facts. Get over this patch of ground as fast as possible and move on.

'King Giorgos gave Christos a dreadful time,' he told her, keeping his voice as neutral as he could. 'Christos and his mother left Khryseis when he was seventeen. Did he tell you he was first in line to the crown of Khryseis's original royal family?'

'No.'

'He was. That's why Giorgos made life hell for him. He made life hard enough for me and I was only second in line. So we both left and made our lives overseas, but when Giorgos died…'

'Giorgos is dead?'

'Without an heir. So Christos should be Crown Prince. It's taken weeks to get this far. To find he was dead. No one on Khryseis knew he'd died.'

'His mother wasn't well when her son died.' He could see facts and emotions swirling, fighting for space as she took in his words. 'I guess… I imagined it was up to her to tell others if she wanted. But she was frail already, and her son's death made things… Well, she died three months later.'

'So Zoe lost her grandmother as well.'

Her eyes flew to his. She hadn't expected that response, he thought, and wondered what she had expected.

'Yes,' she whispered. 'Thank you for recognising that. It did make things much harder.'

'So then you stepped in.'

'There was no one else.'

'And now we have a mess,' he said, choosing his words with care. 'Yes, Christos hated the royal family, but it was King Giorgos he feared and Giorgos's line is finished. The three Diamond Isles have splintered into three principalities. As Christos's only child, Zoe's the new Crown Princess of Khryseis. She'll inherit full sovereign power when she's twenty-five but until then, like it or not, I'm Prince Regent. Whether I want that power or not, the island's desperate for change. The infrastructure's appalling but I only have power for change if Zoe lives on Khryseis for at least three months of every year. Otherwise the power stays with an island council that's as impotent as it is corrupt. Elsa, she has to come home.'

She didn't say a word.

She was a really self-contained woman, he thought. He'd shaken her out of her containment but he'd done it with fear of losing Zoe. She had her self-containment back now, and he had no idea what was going in her head. He wouldn't be privy to it until she decided to speak again.

She poured two tumblers of water. She walked outside—

not limping now, he thought, and found he was relieved. He could cope with an injured child—but not an incapacitated nanny as well. There were two ancient deckchairs on the porch. She sank into one of them and left it to him to decide whether to sit on the other.

The chairs were old and stained and the one left vacant looked to be covered in cat fur.

His trousers were jet-black with a slash of crimson up the side. Ceremonial uniform.

'It brushes off,' she said wryly, not looking at him. Gazing out through the palms to the sea beyond.

He sat.

'You have a cat?' he asked, feeling his way.

'Five,' she said, and as he looked around she shook her head.

'They won't come near when you're here. They're feral cats. Cats are a huge problem up here—they decimate the wildlife. Only Zoe loves them. So we've caught every one we can. If they're at all approachable we have them neutered. We feed them really well at dusk and again in the morning. We lock them up overnight where we feed them—in the little enclosure behind the house. That way they don't need to kill wildlife to eat. Apart from our new little black one, they're fat and lazy, and if you weren't here they'd be lined up here snoozing their day away.'

'You can afford to feed five cats?'

Mistake. Once again she froze. 'You're inordinately interested in my financial affairs,' she said flatly. 'Can you tell me why they're you're business?'

'You're spending Zoe's money.'

'And you're responsible for Zoe how? You didn't even know she existed.'

'Now I do know, she's family.'

'Good, then,' she said. 'Go talk to Zoe's lawyers. They'll tell me we put her money in a trust fund and I take out only what's absolutely necessary for us to live.'

'And the cats?'

She sighed. 'We catch fish,' she said. 'I cook the heads and innards with rice. That's my cat food for the week. So yes, I waste rice and some fish heads on our cats. Shoot me now.'

'I'm not criticising.'

'You are,' she said bluntly. 'You said I'm struggling to care for her. Tell me in what way I'm struggling?'

'Look at this place,' he said before he could stop himself—and her simmering anger exploded.

'I'm looking. I can't see a palace, if that's what you mean. I can't see surround-sound theatre rooms and dishwashers and air-conditioning. I can't see wall to wall carpet and granite bench tops. So how does Zoe need those?'

'It's falling down.'

'So if it falls down I'll rebuild. We have isolation, which Zoe needs until she gets her confidence back. We have our own private beach. We have my work—yes, I'm still doing research and I'm being paid a stipend which goes towards Zoe's medical costs, but...'

'You're paying Zoe's medical costs?'

'Your investigator didn't go very far if he didn't find that out. Her parents hadn't taken out medical insurance,' she said. 'In this country the basics are covered but there have been so many small things. The last lot of plastic surgery was on her shoulder. The surgeon was wonderful—that's why we used him—but he only operates on private patients so we had to pay.'

'*You* had to pay.'

'Whatever.'

'You can't keep doing that.'

'Try and stop me,' she said, carefully neutral again. She'd obviously decided it was important to keep a rein on her temper.

'Where does that leave you?'

'Where I am.'

'Stuck in the middle of nowhere, with a damaged child.'

She put her drink carefully down on the packing case that served as their outdoor table. She rose.

'You know, I'm not enjoying myself here and I have work to do. I correct assignments online and I try to do it while Zoe's asleep. When she wakes we'll drive you back into town. But meanwhile... Meanwhile you go take a walk on the beach, calculate cat food costs, do whatever you want, I don't care. I believe any further dialogue should be through our lawyers.'

And she walked deliberately inside and let the screen door bang closed after her.

CHAPTER FOUR

SHE was true to her word. She wouldn't speak to him until Zoe woke up. He took a walk on the beach, feeling ridiculous in his ridiculous uniform. He came back and talked for a while to a little black cat who deigned to be sociable. Finally Zoe woke, but even then Elsa only spoke when necessary.

'I'll give you the address of my lawyer,' she said.

'I already know who your lawyer is.'

'Of course you do,' she said cordially. 'Silly me.'

'You're being…'

'Obstructive?' she said. 'Yes, I am.'

'What's obstructive?' Zoe asked.

'Not letting your cousin Stefanos have what he wants.'

'What does he want?'

'You might ask him.'

Zoe turned to him, puzzled. 'What do you want?'

'To get to know you,' he said, refusing to be distracted by Elsa's anger. 'Your papa was a very good friend of mine. When he left Khryseis we didn't write—he wanted a clean break. I should have made more of an effort to keep in touch and I'll be sorry for the rest of my life that I didn't. That he married and had a little girl called Zoe…that he died…it breaks my heart that I didn't know.'

'It makes you sad?'

'Very sad.'

But apparently Zoe knew about sad—and she had a cure.

'When I'm in hospital and I'm sad, Elsa tells me about the fish she's seen that day, and shells and starfish. Elsa keeps saying the sea's waiting for me to get well. She brings in pictures of the beach and the house and the cats and she pins them all over the walls so every time I wake up I can see that the sea and this house and our cats are waiting for me.'

His gaze flew to Elsa. She was staring blankly ahead, as if she hadn't heard.

But she had heard, he thought. She surely had.

And he knew then… As he watched her stoical face he realised that he was threatening her foundations. He was threatening to remove a little girl she loved with all her heart.

He'd never thought of this as a possibility. That a nanny could truly love his little cousin.

He'd come here expecting to meet Mrs Elsa Murdoch, paid nanny. Instead he'd met Elsa, marine biologist, friend, protector, mother to Zoe in every sense but name.

After the shock of learning of Zoe's existence, his plan had been to rescue his orphaned cousin, take her back to Khryseis and pay others to continue her care. Or, if Zoe was attached to this particular nanny, then he could continue to employ her to give the kid continuity.

It had to be option two.

Only if he broached it now Elsa might well lock the door and call the authorities to throw him off her land.

So do it when? He had so little time.

'I need to go back to Khryseis tomorrow,' he told Zoe and glanced sideways to see relief flood Elsa's face. 'Elsa's said she'll drive me into town now. But I've upset her. She thought I might want to take you away from her, and I'd never do that. I promise. So if you and Elsa drive me into town now, can I come and visit again tomorrow morning?' He looked ruefully down at his ceremonial trousers—now liberally coated in cat fur. 'If I'm welcome?'

'Is he welcome?' Zoe asked Elsa.

'If you want him to come,' Elsa said neutrally. 'Stefanos is your cousin.'

Zoe thought about it. He was being judged, he thought, and the sensation was weird. Judged by an eight-year-old, with Elsa on the sidelines doing her own judging.

Or…it seemed she'd already judged.

'If you come you should bring your togs,' Zoe said.

'Togs?'

'Your swimming gear—if you own any without tassels and braid,' Elsa said, still obviously forcing herself not to glower. 'As a farewell visit,' she added warningly. 'Because, if you really are Zoe's cousin, then I accept that she should get to know you.'

'That's gracious of you,' he said gravely.

'It is,' she said and managed a half-hearted smile.

The drive back to town started in silence. Elsa's car was an ancient family wagon, filled in the back with—of all things—lobster pots. There was a pile of buoys and nets heaped on the front passenger seat, so he was forced to sit in the rear seat with Zoe.

She could have put the gear in the back, he thought, but she didn't offer and he wasn't pushing it. So she was chauffeur and he and Zoe were passengers.

'You catch lobsters?' he said cautiously.

'We weigh them, sex them, tag then and let them go,' she said briefly from the front.

'You have a boat?'

'The university supplies one. But I only go when Zoe can come with me.'

'It's really fun,' Zoe said. 'I like catching the little ones. You have to be really careful when you pick them up. If you grab them behind their necks they can't reach and scratch you.'

'We have lobsters on the Diamond Isles,' he told her. 'My friend Nikos is a champion fisherman.'

'Do you fish?' Zoe demanded.

'I did when I was a boy.'

They chatted on. Elsa was left to listen. And fret.

He was good, she conceded. He was wriggling his way into

Zoe's trust and that wasn't something lightly achieved. Like her father before her, Zoe was almost excruciatingly shy, and that shyness had been made worse by people's reaction to her scars.

Stefanos hadn't once referred to her scars. To the little girl it must be as if he hadn't noticed them.

The concept, for Zoe, must be huge. Here was someone out of her papa's past, wanting to talk to her about interesting stuff like what he'd done on Khryseis when he was a boy with her papa.

She shouldn't be driving him back into town. She should be asking him to dinner, even asking him to sleep over to give Zoe as much contact as she could get.

Only there were other issues. Like the Crown. Like the fact that he'd said that Zoe had to return to Khryseis. Like crazy stuff that she couldn't consider.

Like asking a prince of the blood whether he'd like to sleep on her living room settee, she thought suddenly, and the idea was so ridiculous she almost smiled.

He was leaving tomorrow. He'd stopped talking about the possibility of Zoe coming with him. Maybe he'd given up.

She glanced into the rear-view mirror and he looked up and met her eyes.

No, she thought, and fear settled back around her heart. Prince Stefanos of Khryseis looked like a man who didn't give up—on anything.

The township of Waratah Cove had two three-star hotels and one luxury six-star resort out on the headland past the town.

Without asking, she turned the car towards the headland and he didn't correct her.

Money, she thought bleakly. If she could have the cost of one night's accommodation in this place…

'Can you stop here?' Stefanos asked and she jammed her foot on the brake and stopped dead. Maybe a bit too suddenly.

'Wow,' Zoe said. 'Are you crabby or something?'

'Or something,' she said neutrally, glancing again at Stefanos in the rear-view mirror.

'Your nanny thinks I spend too much money,' he said, amused, and she flushed. Was she so obvious?

'Elsa's not my nanny,' Zoe said, amused herself.

'What is she?'

'She's just my Elsa.'

My Elsa. It was said with such sureness that he knew he could never break this bond. If he was to take Zoe back to Khryseis, he needed to take them both.

He had to get this right.

'So why did you want me to stop here?' Elsa asked.

'Because the ambassador to the Diamond Isles leaked to the media that I was coming here,' he said bitterly. 'That's why I had to find myself a uniform and attend the reception. I've already had to bribe—heavily—the chauffeur they arranged for me so he wouldn't tell anyone my location. I imagine there'll be cameramen outside my hotel, wanting to know where I've been, and I don't want a media circus descending on Zoe. I can walk the last couple of hundred yards.'

'Maybe you should check your trousers,' Elsa said, and there was suddenly laughter in her voice. 'Cat fur isn't a great look for a Royal Prince.'

'Thanks very much,' he said, and smiled.

And, unaccountably, she smiled back.

Hers was a gorgeous smile. Warm and natural and full of humour. If he'd met this woman under normal circumstances...

Maybe he'd never have noticed her, he thought. She didn't move in the circles he moved in. Plus he liked his women groomed. Sophisticated. Able to hold their own in any company.

She'd be able to hold her own. This was one feisty woman.

He needed to learn more about her. He needed to hit the phones, extend his research, come up with an offer she couldn't refuse.

Unaccountably, he didn't want to get out of the car. The

battered family wagon, loaded with lobster pots, smelling faintly—no, more than faintly—of fish, unaccountably seemed a good place to stay.

He thought suddenly of his apartment in Manhattan. Of his consulting suite with its soft grey carpet, its trendy chrome furniture, its soft piped music.

They were worlds apart—he and Mrs Elsa Murdoch.

But now their lives needed to overlap, enough to keep the island safe. The islanders safe.

Zoe safe.

Until today he'd seen Zoe as a problem—a shock, to be muted before the islanders found out.

Now, suddenly that obstacle was human—a little girl with scars, attached to a woman who loved her.

They were waiting for him to get out of the car. If he left it any longer a media vehicle might come this way. One cameraman and Zoe would run, he thought, and it'd be Elsa who ran with her.

Elsa wasn't family. It wasn't her role to care for Zoe.

Forget the roles, he told himself sharply. Now he must protect the pair of them. He climbed from the car and tried to dust himself off. He had ginger cat fur on black trousers.

Suddenly Elsa was out of the car as well, watching as he shrugged on his jacket.

'Do your buttons up,' she said, almost kindly. 'You look much more princely with your buttons done up. And hold still. If a car comes I'll stop, but let's see what we can achieve before that happens.'

And, before he knew what she intended, she'd twisted him round so she could attack the backs of his legs and the seat of his trousers.

With a hairbrush?

'It's actually a brush Zoe uses for her dolls,' she told him, sweeping the cat fur off in long efficient strokes. 'But see— I've rolled sticky tape the wrong way round around its bristles. It's very effective.'

He was so confounded he submitted. He was standing on

a headland in the middle of nowhere while a woman called Mrs Elsa Murdoch attacked his trousers with a dolls' hairbrush.

She brushed until she was satisfied. Then she straightened. 'Turn round and let me look at you,' she said.

He turned.

'Very nice,' she said. 'Back to being a prince again. What do you think, Zoe? Is he ready for the cameras?'

'His top button's undone,' Zoe said.

'That's because it's hot,' he retorted but Elsa shook her head.

'No class at all,' she said soulfully. 'I don't know what you modern day royals are coming to.' She carefully fastened his top button while he felt…he felt… He didn't know how he felt; he was only aware that when the button was fastened and she stepped back there was a sharp stab of something that might even be loss.

'There you go, Your Highness,' she said, like a valet who'd just done a good job making a recalcitrant prince respectable. 'Off you go and face the world while Zoe and I get back to our cats and our lobster pots.'

And she was in the car, turned and driving away before he had a chance to reply.

His first task was to get his breath back. To face the media with some sort of dignity.

His second task was to talk to the hotel concierge.

'I need some extensive shopping done on my behalf,' he said. 'Fast. Oh, and I need to hire a car. No, not a limousine. Anything not smelling of fish would be acceptable.'

Then he rang Prince Alexandros back in the Diamond Isles. As well as being a friend, Alexandros was Crown Prince of Sappheiros, and Alex more than anyone else knew what was at stake—why he was forced to be in Australia in royal uniform when he should be in theatre garb back in Manhattan.

'Problem?' his friend asked.

'I don't know.'

'What don't you know?'

'The child's been burned. She's dreadfully scarred.'

There was a sharp intake of breath. 'Hell. Is she…'

'She's okay. It's healing. But my idea of leaving her on the island… She'll have special needs.'

'You were never going to be able to leave her anyway.'

'I don't have a choice,' he snapped. 'You know I can't leave my work yet—I can't break promises. But there's a nanny. A good one. A Mrs Elsa Murdoch. She's not like any Mrs Elsa Murdoch I've ever met.'

There was a lengthy silence on the end of the phone. Then, 'How many Mrs Elsa Murdochs have you met?' Alexandros asked, with a certain amount of caution.

Uh-oh. Alex and Stefanos had known each other since they were kids. Maybe Alex had heard something in his voice that he didn't necessarily want to share.

'Just the one,' he said.

Another silence. 'She's young?' Alex ventured.

'Yes.'

'Aha.'

'There's no aha about it.'

'There's a Mr Elsa Murdoch?'

'No.'

'I rest my case,' he said. 'Hey, Stefanos, like me, you've spent so much of your life pushing your career…avoiding family. Maybe it's time you did a heads up and noticed the Elsa Murdochs of this world.'

'Alex…' He couldn't think what to add next.

'You want something more?' Alex asked. 'Something specific? If not…my wife's waiting for me. Not a bad thing for a prince to have, you know. A wife. Especially if that prince needs to care for a child with injuries.'

'This isn't a joke.'

'I don't believe I was joking,' Alex threw back at him. 'Okay, so this Mrs Elsa Murdoch… You want to tell me about her?'

How had he got himself into this conversation? He didn't have a clue.

'I'll leave you to your wife,' he said stiffly.

'Excellent,' Alex said. 'I'll leave you to your Mrs Elsa Murdoch. And your little Crown Princess. Steve…'

'Yes?'

'Take care. And keep an open mind. Speaking as a man who's just married…it can make all the difference in the world.'

Elsa lay awake far into the night, staring at a life she'd never envisaged. A life without Zoe.

She'd never thought of it.

Four years ago she'd been happily married, full of plans for the future, working with Matty and her good friends and their little girl.

One stupid drunken driver—who'd walked away unscathed—and she was left with nothing but the care of Zoe.

Up until today she'd thought Zoe depended totally on her. Up until now she'd never really considered that the reverse was true as well.

Without Zoe…

No. She couldn't think it. It left a void in her life so huge it terrified her.

He'd backed off. He'd said he was leaving tomorrow.

Zoe's needed back on Khryseis.

She reran his words through her mind—she remembered almost every word he'd uttered. He hadn't backed off.

Zoe's needed back on Khryseis.

She was Zoe's legal guardian. But if it came to a custody battle between Elsa, with no blood tie and no means of giving Zoe the last operations she so desperately needed—or Stefanos, a royal prince, a blood relative, with money and means at his disposal, able to give her every chance in life…

What choice was there?

She felt sick and tired.

A letter lay on her bureau. She rose from her tumbled

sheets—lying in bed was useless anyway—and read it for the thousandth time.

It was an outline of costs for cosmetic plastic surgery to smooth the skin under Zoe's chin and across her neck.

She'd sold everything she had. There was no money left.

Stefanos.

Not if it meant losing Zoe. Not!

Who was she protecting here? Herself or Zoe?

Damn him!

She should be welcoming him, she thought. Knight on white charger with loaded wallet.

Not if it meant giving up Zoe.

To watch them go…

To watch him go.

Where had that thought come from? Nowhere. She did not need to think he was sexy. The fact that he was drop-dead gorgeous only added to her fear. She did not need her hormones to stir.

They were stirring.

She walked outside, stood on the veranda and stared into the dark.

Prince Stefanos of Khryseis. Cousin to Zoe.

A man about to change her life.

A man about to take her child.

Fifteen miles across the water, Stefanos was doing the same thing. Watching the moonbeams ripple across the ocean. Thinking how his life had changed.

Because of Zoe.

And…Elsa? A barefoot, poverty stricken marine biologist of a nanny?

He had a million other things to think about.

So why was he thinking of Elsa?

It was mid-morning when he arrived and they hadn't left for the beach yet. There was a tiny seeping wound under Zoe's arm. It was minuscule but they'd learned from bitter experience to treat small as big. This was a skin graft area. If it extended Zoe could lose the whole graft—an appalling prospect.

Elsa had found it while she was applying Zoe's suncream and now she was hovering between wait and see or ring the local medical centre and get it seen to now.

Only it was Sunday. Their normal doctor would be away. Waratah Cove had a small bush-nursing hospital, manned by casual staff over the weekend. Less experienced doctors tended to react to Zoe's injuries with fear, dreading under-treating. If she took Zoe in, she'd be admitted and transferred to hospital in the city. Simple as that.

And they were both so weary of hospitals.

Her worry almost made her forget Stefanos was coming—but not completely. The sound of a car on the track made her feel as if the world was caving in, landing right on her shoulders.

She hated this. She just hated it.

She tugged a T-shirt over Zoe's scarred little body and turned to welcome him. And almost gasped.

This was a different Stefanos. Faded jeans. T-shirt. Scuffed trainers.

Great body. Really great body.

A body to make her feel she was a woman again.

She had to do something about these hormones. They were doing things to her head. She'd married Matty. His picture was still on the mantel. Get a grip.

'Hi,' he said, and smiled at the two of them and Elsa couldn't resist. She had to smile. It was as if he had the strength to change her world, just by smiling.

'Hi,' Zoe said shyly and smiled as well, and Elsa looked at Zoe in astonishment. Two minutes earlier the two of them had been close to tears.

Stefanos's smile was a force to be reckoned with.

'I thought you'd be at the beach,' he said, and then he looked more closely—maybe seeing the traces of their distress. 'Is something wrong?'

'We thought we wouldn't go to the beach this morning,' Elsa said repressively. Zoe loathed people talking about her injuries. She'd had enough fuss to last one small girl a lifetime.

Stefanos had never mentioned her scars. Maybe he hadn't even noticed. Or…not.

'Why not?' he said gently, and suddenly he was talking to Zoe, and not to her. As if he'd guessed.

'There's a bit of my skin graft come loose,' Zoe said.

Once again it was as much as Elsa could do not to gasp. Zoe never volunteered such information.

She'd had the best doctors—the best!—but almost every one of them talked to her and not to Zoe. Oh, they chatted to Zoe, but in the patronising way elders often talked to children. For the hard questions—even things like: 'Is she sleeping at night?'—they turned to her, as if Zoe couldn't possibly know.

So what had Stefanos done different?

She knew. He hadn't treated her as an object of sympathy, and he'd talked directly to her. Simple but so important.

'Whereabouts?' Stefanos asked, still speaking only to Zoe.

'Under my arm at the back.'

'Is it hurting?'

'No, but…it's scary,' Zoe said, and her bottom lip wobbled.

'Can I ask why?'

'Elsa will have to take me to hospital and they'll make me stay there, and I don't want to go.' Her voice ended on a wail, she turned her face into Elsa's shirt and she sobbed.

'Zoe,' Stefanos said, in a voice she'd not heard before. Gentle, yet firm. He squatted so he was at her eye level. 'Zoe, will you let me take a look? I don't know if I can help, but I'm a doctor. Will you trust me to see if I think you need hospital?'

He was a doctor?

There was a loaded silence. Zoe would be as stunned as she was, Elsa thought.

You still can't have her, she thought, her instinctive response overriding everything else, but she had the sense to shut up. The last thing Zoe needed was more fear.

Because, astonishingly, Zoe was turning towards him. She was still hard against Elsa but he'd cut through her distress.

'You're a doctor?'

'Yes.'

'But you're a prince.'

'People are allowed to be both.'

'My papa was a doctor,' she said. 'But a doctor of science. He studied shellfish.'

'Did Christos get his doctorate?' he said with pleasure. 'Hey, how about that. I wish I'd known.' Still he was talking to Zoe. 'Your papa and I used to be really good friends. He taught me where to find the best shells on Khryseis. Only I always wanted to find the pretty ones or the big ones and he wanted to look for the interesting ones. Sometimes he'd pick up a little grey shell I didn't think at all special and off he'd go, telling me it was a Multi-Armpit Hairy Cyclamate, or a Wobblysaurus Rex, or something even sillier.'

Zoe stared in astonishment—and then she giggled.

You could forgive a lot of a man who could make Zoe giggle, Elsa conceded. And…a man who could make her giggle as well?

'Will you let me see what the problem is?' he asked gently, and Zoe lifted her T-shirt without hesitation. Which was another miracle all by itself.

And here was another miracle. He didn't react. Zoe's left side was a mass of scar tissue but Stefanos's expression didn't change by as much as a hair's breadth. He was still smiling a little—with Zoe—and she was smiling back. His long fingers probed the scar tissue with infinite gentleness, not going near the tiny suppurating wound but simply assessing the situation overall.

He had such long fingers, Elsa thought. Big hands, tanned and gentle. She wouldn't mind…

Um…whoa. Attention back to Zoe. Fast.

'What sort of medical supplies do you have here?' he asked, still speaking only to Zoe, and Elsa held her breath.

This was a question every doctor or nurse she knew would address to her, but this whole conversation was between the two of them.

'We have lots of stuff,' Zoe volunteered. 'Sometimes when I'm just out of hospital the nurses come here and change my dressings. It costs a lot though, 'cause we're so far out of town, so Elsa keeps a lot of stuff here and she's learned to do it instead.'

'Well, good for Elsa.' And, dumbly, Elsa found she was blushing with pleasure. 'Can I see?' he asked.

'I'll get it,' she said and headed for the bathroom—and even that was a minor miracle. For Zoe to let her leave the room while a strange doctor was examining her... Definitely a miracle.

She didn't push it, though. She was back in seconds, carrying a hefty plastic crate. She set it down and Stefanos examined its contents and whistled.

'You have enough here to treat an elephant,' he said. 'You don't have an elephant hidden under a bed somewhere, do you?'

Once again Zoe giggled. It was the best sound. It made her feel... It made her feel...

No. She would not get turned on because this man made a child giggle.

Only she already was. She was fighting hormones here as hard as she could. And losing.

It had been too long. You're a sick, sad spinster, she told herself, and then rebuked herself sharply. Not a spinster. She glanced across at the mantel, and Matty's face smiled down at her from its frame. Sorry, she told him under her breath. Sorry, sorry, sorry.

'You know, I'm sure I can fix this.' Stefanos's words tugged her attention straight back to him. 'Zoe, if you and Elsa trust me... I think all this needs is some antiseptic cream, a couple of Steri-Strips to tug it together—see, it's at the end of the graft so we can attach the strips to good skin on either side and tug it together. Then we can pop one of these water-proof dressings over the whole thing and you could even go swimming this morning. Which, seeing I brought my bathers, is probably a good thing.' He grinned.

And Elsa thought, I'm in trouble here. I'm in serious trouble.

But they were moving on. Stefanos rose and washed his hands with the thoroughness of a surgeon. Then he lifted Zoe carefully—being mindful of where her scars were without Zoe noticing he was mindful, Elsa thought. He sat her on the kitchen table and proceeded to do his stuff.

He was skilled. She just had to see those fingers gently probing. She just had to listen to him chat to Zoe, distracting her as he worked. He was so careful, so precise, and she thought of all the doctors who'd treated Zoe over the past four years and she thought this man was a blessing.

This man wanted to take Zoe away.

This man was Zoe's cousin—a prince.

This man was a doctor, with all the skills needed to take care of her.

She was a marine biologist with nothing.

He was applying the waterproof dressing now and he glanced over his shoulder to say something to her. And he saw her expression. She'd tried to get it under control but he could see—she knew he could see.

'There's nothing to be afraid of, Elsa,' he said gently and she thought, You don't know the half of it. Nothing to be afraid of? When he was threatening to turn her world around?

'I… You came here to talk,' she said, and it was really hard to get her words out.

'I came here to swim,' he said. 'Are there any other problems to sort before we swim? Nothing I can treat? Ingrown toenails? Snakebite? Measles?'

Zoe giggled again and wriggled down from the table. She was totally at ease now, completely relaxed in his company.

He couldn't take her away, she thought frantically. Zoe would always want her. Wouldn't she?

There's nothing to be afraid of, she told herself, but she knew she was lying.

There was everything to be afraid of. Everything she held dear.

But for now…it seemed they were going for a swim.

CHAPTER FIVE

THE swim was glorious, fun and deeply scary.

Glorious in that the weather gods had decided this was another day out of the box—brilliant sunshine but not too hot, the water cool enough to refresh but not so cold they couldn't stay in for as long they wanted, turquoise-clear so they could see everything on the bottom.

Fun because Stefanos made it fun. He twisted and turned under the water, teaching Zoe new tricks, tickling her toes on the sandy bottom, making her play as a child should play. As Zoe had been unable to play.

She'd been isolated for so long. She should be with other children, but there were so many complications. Twice Elsa had tried to send her to school but each time she'd ended up with a major infection and back in hospital.

So if it couldn't be a bunch of kids whooping and hollering around her, Stefanos was definitely next best. He was a fabulous swimmer and he knew how to make Zoe laugh.

Of course he was and of course he did, Elsa thought, with what she recognised as dumb and irrational resentment. She loved that Zoe was falling for Stefanos's charm, but she was also fearful of it.

She was fearful of falling for Stefanos's charm herself.

Because he was…gorgeous. She'd seen him yesterday in full royal regalia and thought he was gorgeous then. She'd seen him this morning in his jeans and T-shirt and thought he was just plain yummy. Now, clad only in his board shorts, she could hardly keep her eyes off him. Lean and tanned, every muscle delineated…

He was a doctor, for heaven's sake. He must spend his life indoors. Where had he got those muscles?

He was scaring her. Not only because of what he'd suggested yesterday—that he take Zoe away. Not only because of his effect on Zoe. But because of his effect on her.

Mathew had been dead for four years now. Her friends told her it was time to move on.

She'd never had the slightest urge to move on, until right now. And now…what her body was telling her, what her hormones were telling her, felt like a betrayal.

'Mathew, Mathew, Mathew,' she murmured over and over, and because Zoe was perfectly safe with her big cousin, because Stefanos's sole desire seemed to be to make the little girl laugh, she left them to it, stroking strongly out across the entrance to the cove.

She put her head down and swam as she never swam, for it wasn't safe to do this when no one was here to watch Zoe. She'd always gloried in swimming. It was her quiet time. Her time of peace. She was swimming now, hoping her head could settle, so her jumbled thoughts could somehow untangle, so she could find the strength to stand up to this unknown prince and his terrifying charm.

She lost track of time. She swam and swam and finally when she raised her head she realised Zoe and Stefanos were out of the water, standing on the beach and watching her.

And that felt strange too. That this man was watching her…

She caught a wave back to the beach, surfing in with the agility she'd always gloried in. The sea had always been her escape. It could be again, she thought. If the worst happened. If he took Zoe away…

They strolled down the beach to meet her. Her wave washed her into the shallows, she wiped her eyes and looked up to find Stefanos standing above her, smiling, holding out his hand to tug her up.

She nearly didn't take it, she was so disconcerted. But that'd be petty. Zoe was standing beside him, beaming, waiting for her to stand.

She took his hand, he tugged her up and she came up too fast.

She stumbled and he steadied her. Which was a tiny gesture—Prince steadies Elsa—and why the feel of his hands on her waist should have the power to totally disconcert her she didn't know.

'You're beautiful,' he said and she was disconcerted all over again.

'Do you…' She fought for breath and took a while finding it. 'Do you mind?'

'I'm only speaking the truth.'

'Right,' she said and headed up the beach fast. She grabbed her towel and disappeared underneath. At least here she could get her face under control.

Beautiful?

Matty had thought she was beautiful. Until then no one. After him no one.

She wasn't even wearing a bathing suit. Neither she nor Zoe did. They both wore shorts and T-shirts. It'd be unfair for her to wear pretty bathers when Zoe had to wear scar-covering clothes. And she had scars herself—nothing like Zoe's, but bad enough.

And besides, she thought grimly, she was mousy. She'd always been mousy and she always would be mousy. Mathew had thought she was beautiful because he'd fallen in love with her mind. He'd been academically brilliant and he'd loved that she could keep up with him. Her intelligence was a turn on.

But her body? Not so much that he'd ever said. Beauty was in the eye of the beholder and in Mathew's eyes she was his brilliant wife.

Matty.

Dammit, why wasn't he here? And…why was he starting to fade? It was terrifying that when she thought of him now the image that came straight to mind was the photograph on the mantel. Photographs were becoming the reality, and reality moved on, whether she willed it or not.

All this she thought under her towel. All this she thought while she rubbed her hair dry.

'Zoe and I think your hair will dry faster in the sun.'

His voice made her jump. They'd followed her up the beach!

You're not being paranoid? she demanded of herself, and she knew that she was.

'It's lunch time,' Zoe said, puzzled. 'You never take this long to dry your hair.'

And I never have a Prince of the Blood waiting to see when I'll come out from my towel, she thought, but what the heck, there was no choice.

She emerged. She wrapped her towel around her hair and she checked on Zoe. Another surprise. She was wrapped sarong-style in her towel.

'You're dry.'

'Stefanos dried me,' she said. 'And he was really careful of my scars.'

Once again, a jolt. Here was another adult with the responsibility and skills to help her look after this injured child.

If he lived down the road she'd welcome him with open arms.

He lived on the Diamond Isles. Khryseis. A world away from her world.

'Lunch,' he said, smiling at her, and there was a trace of sympathy in his smile that said he understood her turmoil. He couldn't help it, he couldn't stop it, but he understood.

How could you understand? she thought. You're not having her. You're not!

What had he said? *There's nothing to be afraid of.*

Did she believe him?

No way.

＊＊＊

Lunch was the same as yesterday, only Zoe ate more without being prodded. Then Stefanos disappeared to his car and returned with a box.

Cherries! She'd seen them in the shops last week. They'd been twenty dollars a small box, and they'd still been hard, not fully ripened. These were almost the size of golf balls, deep burgundy, shining and luscious.

Stefanos was looking smug—deeply pleased with the fact that her jaw and Zoe's jaw had dropped to somewhere round their ankles. 'The concierge at my hotel knows someone who flies up here from wherever cherries grow,' he told them. 'They're hot off the plane.'

Twenty dollars wouldn't pay for transport from the airport, Elsa thought. How much had these cost?

'They're not to be wasted,' he said severely, and Zoe needed no further prodding. She popped one into her mouth really fast.

'They're not just for eating,' he told her, lifting two pairs of cherries, each pair joined at the stem, and looping them over Zoe's ears. 'Cherry earrings are my favourite accessory.'

'You wear them too,' Zoe said, and he promptly did.

A prince was sitting at her kitchen table wearing cherry earrings.

Her foundations were getting shaky.

'Have a cherry,' he said kindly. 'They go off fast, I hear.'

'Not in range of us, they don't,' she said and ate a cherry and then another. And then...why not?...another.

'I'm up to nine already,' Zoe crowed. Zoe was showered and shiny clean, her face was flushed with pleasure and she was popping cherries in with an enjoyment Elsa had never seen. For four long years, for operation after operation, this little girl had been cheated of her childhood. And now... Stefanos had arrived and joy was flooding in.

Without warning, tendrils of fear wound their way round her heart yet again. But this time it was different. It wasn't just the fear of Zoe being taken away. It was stronger. Maybe Stefanos could give Zoe a better life than she could. If he cared for his little cousin and loved her and made her laugh… What right did she have to stand in his way?

'You're not eating,' he said gently and draped cherry earrings on her as well. 'There. We're the cherry family— Mama Cherry, Papa Cherry, Baby Cherry.'

She smiled and ate another cherry but there were icicles forming inside. She'd only ever wanted what was best for Zoe. If this was what was best…

'Let me show you what else I have in my car,' he said, watching her face. He could see her terror, she thought. This man saw things she didn't want to reveal to anyone.

Maybe it was the man himself who terrified her the most.

'Presents?' Zoe said hopefully and he grinned.

'Exactly,' he said. 'Coming right up.'

'This is exciting,' Zoe said.

'It is.' She was desperately trying to match Zoe's pleasure. Outwardly succeeding. Inwardly failing.

And then he was back, carrying suitcases, one soft blue leather, the other pink.

Suitcases. A wave of nausea swept over her so strongly that she rose and made a move towards the bathroom.

Stefanos dumped the suitcases and stopped her.

'Elsa, no,' he said softly. 'I told you before, you have nothing to be afraid of.'

'You're taking Zoe away.' She hadn't meant to say it. To say it in front of Zoe was unforgivable, but her terror was too raw, too real for her to disguise it.

'I do need to take Zoe to Khryseis,' he said, still in that gentle, reassuring tone that must surely be a learned bedside manner. *Yes, we are going to elongate your ears and swap your legs for your arms, but trust me, I'm a doctor.*

'Trust me,' he said now, as Zoe rose, her panic matching Elsa's. 'I want to take you both to the Diamond Isles. Zoe is the Crown Princess of Khryseis. Khryseis needs Zoe, and Zoe needs you. So I need you both. Thus I'm asking if you'll both come home with me.'

* * *

It was important—really important—to get her expression right. Zoe was staring at her and she'd seen terror. Stefanos was Zoe's cousin. This was Zoe's life, not hers. She had to get fear off her face and show courage.

'You…you scared me,' she managed at last, and to her relief her voice came out calm. 'I saw the suitcase and I thought you might be wanting Zoe to go away today. She doesn't even have a passport.'

'It will take a few days to get the documentation through.' His gaze was holding hers. 'Zoe, I think I frightened Elsa,' he said, rueful. 'How can we stop her being scared?'

You could go away, Elsa thought, but she knew Zoe wouldn't say that. Zoe was entranced with her big new cousin, and why shouldn't she be?

Stefanos was a prince, Zoe was a princess, and he'd pulled Zoe onside simply by acting as if the two of them needed to reassure her. Prince and princess together.

'Hey, Elsa, it's okay,' he said and reached to take her hand. His hold was strong and firm and…reassuring? How could touch be reassuring? How could his touch warm her when she was so cold she was beginning to shake?

She should pull away.

She couldn't.

'Does Khryseis have a beach?' Zoe asked, and Elsa knew right then that this was a done deal. 'Elsa likes beaches,' the little girl told her cousin. 'We looked at Khryseis on the computer and Elsa said she bet there were more fish than we could count. And more starfish.'

'Starfish?' he said, bemused, and his hand was still holding hers. She should pull it away, but how could she? How could she find strength to pull from such a touch?

'The real name for starfish is echinoderms, or asteroidea,' Zoe was saying importantly. 'They have two stomachs. They use one stomach to digest food while the other stomach turns inside out to pull its food in. But the really cool thing is that if they lose an arm they can grow another one. If I was a starfish I could grow another finger. And if you find just one leg of a starfish still joined to just a little bit of its body, a whole new starfish can grow. How cool is that?'

'Really cool,' he said, sounding stunned.

'It's what me and Elsa are working on,' she told him, sounding about twenty years older than her eight years. 'And the Internet says Khryseis has some really weird starfish.' She turned to Elsa, her eyes shining with small girl excitement. 'Elsa, can we go?'

No, she wanted to scream. No!

Instead she took a deep breath. She tried a tug on her hand but it wasn't released.

'Sweetheart, maybe we could work things out so you could go,' she whispered. 'I need to work.'

Zoe's face fell. 'I can't go without you,' she said, her bottom lip wobbling. 'I'd be scared.'

So would I, Elsa thought, but once again she held her tongue.

'I need you both to come,' Stefanos said. He was watching the two of them, focusing as much on Elsa as he was on Zoe. The pressure on her hand remained. Was he trying to warn her? she wondered. It didn't feel like that. It simply felt as if he was feeding her...strength. It was a crazy concept but it seemed the only one that would fit.

'That's why I've brought two suitcases,' he told them. Finally he released her hand. He'd set the suitcases on the floor and he flipped one open.

From the top he lifted a shiny new laptop computer. She'd seen these advertised. They were worth...a tenth of Zoe's next operation?

'This is for you,' he told her, setting it on the table. 'Whether you decide to come or not. You work from home. Why can't that home be on Khryseis?'

Because...

There was no because. She couldn't think of one, apart from the fact that the thought left her terrified.

She glanced at the mantel. Mathew's face smiled at her. Steadied her.

There must be a because.

Because my husband is buried here? Because this is where my grief is?

That wasn't a good because.

Because this guy in front of me makes my body react as I don't believe it's ever reacted?

Well, that was something she needed to dismiss. How weak a because was that?

Because I'd have no control over Zoe's life? Because people would stare at her scars? Because, as a royal, she'd be on display, and it could well destroy her?

Here at last were valid reasons, but before she could voice them Stefanos had lifted parcels onto the table.

'These are for you,' he said softly to Zoe. 'Because you're one of the bravest young women I've met. Because I know how much your body's hurt over the last four years, and I know how beautiful you are, inside and out. I'm so sorry I wasn't here for you when your parents died but I am now. These are to make you even more beautiful than you already are.'

Zoe looked uncertainly at Elsa—and then tentatively unwrapped the top parcel.

It was a pink blouse. It had tiny buttons shaped like butterflies. It had soft puffed sleeves designed to reach Zoe's elbows. A tiny white mandarin collar was designed so the top buttons could stay open, but the collar itself would stay high. Just high enough to hide the scars.

And there was more.

Elsa had searched for clothes like these, as far as her budget could afford it. She'd even tried making them. That was a joke, trying to learn dressmaking from an instruction manual. To say her attempts had failed was an understatement.

But after one night Stefanos had found these. There were three pairs of trousers, capri style, like long shorts, one red and white, one a lovely soft blue and one a deeper shade of pink. There were four more blouses, each with the same soft high collar. There were hair ribbons to match, and pretty sandals and a couple of dainty bracelets. There was an exquisite lilac party dress with white lace and a vast bow at the back. It came with a lilac choker with stars embroidered in white.

Within minutes Zoe was surrounded by a sea of clothes. She looked up at Elsa and her eyes were shining.

'They're beautiful,' she breathed. 'Can I keep them?'

What sort of question was that? There was no way she could refuse this gift. She just wished, so badly it hurt, that she'd been in a position to give these to her herself.

'They might not fit,' Stefanos warned, casting Elsa a thoughtful glance and then directing his attention back to Zoe. 'I had to guess sizes, but I've organised a dressmaker to visit you this evening and let them out or take them in as you need. We can change anything too—she has my authority.'

'And my authority?' Elsa whispered.

'I hope you'll agree,' Stefanos said gravely and met her gaze and held.

What was she thinking? 'Of course I agree,' she said shakily. She hugged Zoe and managed a smile. 'They're lovely. Your cousin has been wonderfully generous.' She bit her lip. 'But you're not my cousin, Stefanos. I can't take the laptop.'

'It's part of a debt,' he said softly. 'I owe you so much.'

'You owe me nothing.'

'I loved Christos.'

'He was my friend too.'

'No,' he said, and suddenly he was almost stern. 'You don't understand. Christos was my family. That I didn't know he was dead…that Zoe has been alone for so long…it touches my honour. I'm asking you to take this and it doesn't begin to repay the debt I owe you.'

It touches my honour… It was a quaint phrase. Old-fashioned.

He meant it—absolutely.

'I…' She took a deep breath. If they were going to talk about old-fashioned… 'Then it's my honour to care for Zoe,' she said, and she tilted her chin. 'Zoe is not related to me by blood, but I'm her godmother and her guardian. I won't let that go.'

'I'm not asking you to,' he said evenly. 'I'm asking for you to give Khryseis a chance. I'm asking you to come with Zoe—as her nanny as well as her guardian—and if you do this then you *will* be paid. I want you to help me introduce her to her birthright.'

'And then come home without her?'

'No,' Zoe said. She'd been examining her pile of clothes with joy, but this wasn't a child who could be bought. She looked at the clothes with longing and then pushed them away. Suddenly panicking. 'I don't want them if I can't have Elsa.'

'You can have Elsa,' Stefanos said evenly. 'I'm asking you both to come.' He smiled at Elsa, ignoring her obvious panic, simply smiling at her as if he understood what she was thinking; she was being slightly foolish but he wasn't about to threaten her.

His smile lied, she thought desperately. This man was a prince, about as far from her world as it was possible to be. He was accustomed to having his charm work for him. He thought now that he simply had to smile and shower gifts and he'd get what he wanted.

'Do you know what a royal nanny earns?' he asked, and she caught her breath.

'I don't want to know.'

'Now that's just dumb,' he said. 'Knocking back a fabulous job because you haven't heard the terms? I rang a couple of friends last night. They have nannies in Europe and they kindly rang a couple of the top agencies and asked. What's the going rate for the best nanny in the world? they asked.'

And he gave her a figure.

She gasped. She stared across the table at him and he smiled back at her. 'That's what I'm offering,' he said softly. 'Starting today.'

She could be paid for doing what she loved? Caring for Zoe?

But this… This could never be about money. Because she did what she did for Zoe for love; for nothing else.

'Elsa, Zoe needs to come home anyway,' he said gently. 'I'm sorry, but it's not negotiable. I've also talked to people here in Social Services and to lawyers from your Family Court. I have more chance at success in gaining custody than you might think. The court would look at what Zoe stands to inherit. They'd look at the home I'm prepared to give her. The consensus is that she should have the right to learn about Khryseis. It's her heritage.'

He turned to Zoe and spread his hands. 'Zoe, your father was the Crown Prince of Khryseis and you're now the Crown Princess. If you agree, I'd like to show you the place where your papa grew up. I'd like to introduce you to an island that I know you'll love, to live in a palace that's exciting, to see what your father's life could have been if he'd lived. I'm asking Elsa to come as well, and I'd like you both to consider Khryseis as a place to live.' He glanced at Elsa and then glanced away. Her emotions were written on her face, she thought.

'I'll sign legal documents with international legal author-ities,' he said, and now he was speaking directly to Elsa. 'We need Zoe for at least three months a year.'

'For ever?' Elsa whispered.

'Until Zoe's old enough to know whether she wishes to accept the Crown,' he said and suddenly he sounded stern. 'It's her birthright, Elsa, and neither of us have the right to take that away from her.'

She was close to tears—but she would not cry. Not in front of Zoe. Zoe was taking her cues from her—to disintegrate on her own behalf would be cruel.

And he knew what she was thinking.

'Hey, it's not so bad. You could think of it as a holiday.' He took her hands again. Strong and warm and sure. 'You've been on your own for so long, Elsa. Will you let me share?'

She would not cry. But the feel of his hands…

You've been on your own for so long…

That was what it felt like. Four long years of fighting to get Zoe the medical treatment she needed, fighting to keep her own career viable enough to put food on the table, fighting to forget the ache in her hip and to stop the grey fog of depression and loneliness taking her over.

A holiday in Khryseis. Three months a year?

If she said yes, she'd lose Zoe.

'You won't lose her,' Stefanos said, strongly and surely. 'I promise you that. I've spent the last eighteen hours finding out exactly what you've done for Zoe. The money you've spent. Your own money.'

Her eyes flew to his. Distress gave way to indignation. 'How did you find that out? Who are you to…?'

'To enquire? I have friends in high places, Elsa. So does Zoe now. In future she'll have the best medical treatment money can buy.'

Anger, fear, anguish… They were a kaleidoscope of her emotions. But they should be her emotions. Not Zoe's. This was Zoe's future and she must not deny her.

Her own terror had to be put aside.

'What do you think, Zoe?' she asked, feeling inordinately pleased when she got her voice right. 'Stefanos is offering us an initial three-month holiday on his island while we see what it's like. It's been…it's been a shock, but I don't think it's something we should be scared of. His island looks really beautiful on the Internet.'

'It's *your* island, Zoe,' Stefanos said, gently but firmly.

'So let me get this right,' Elsa said, opening the laptop to give her something to look at rather than Stefanos's face. He saw too much, she thought. He knew how scared she was and he was sympathetic. But still he was determined.

She couldn't afford to be seduced into doing what was wrong for Zoe.

Seduced? It was the wrong word but it was the one that popped into her head. Because…because…

Because he was too big and too male and too sexy and she'd

been alone for far too long. It felt dangerous to even be in the same room as him.

Maybe *he* should be worried, she thought dryly. If he knew what this scary, ridiculous part of her was thinking...

Nanny jumps prince...

Whoa.

Well, at least that pulled her out of the fog, she decided, fighting an almost hysterical desire to laugh. Maybe she ought to focus on slightly more...realistic issues.

'Let me get this straight,' she said again, and watched him smile. How much of what she was thinking was obvious? To her fury she felt a blush start, from the toes up.

'Christos...Zoe's papa...should have been Crown Prince of Khryseis,' she managed, staring fiercely down at the laptop as if she was totally absorbed in its keyboard. 'How come the King wasn't his father?'

Stefanos nodded, still serious. 'Potted history? The Diamond Isles were principalities for hundreds of years,' he told her. 'Then the Prince of Sappheiros invaded the other islands and declared himself King. Subsequent armies kept the islanders under iron rule, and his line continued as long as there was a direct male heir. Six generations later, King Giorgos died without a son. The islands have continued supporting their own royal families, even though they haven't been able to publicly acknowledge them, and now they can take their rightful place. Giorgos's death meant Christos was heir to the throne of Khryseis. Under the old rule, men and women inherited equally. Therefore Zoe inherits after Christos. As her closest adult relative I'm Prince Regent until she can take the throne at twenty-five. Currently the island's being run by a council set up by Giorgos. They're corrupt and useless. The only way for us to unseat them is for Zoe to come home and for us to take over.'

'Us?'

'I was thinking me,' he said, suddenly converting from history lesson to the personal. 'But in the long-term...' He smiled at her, considering. 'Maybe you can find a way to be useful as well.'

'Useful?' The concept made Elsa gasp. What was she letting herself in for? This man...this *prince*...was moving way too fast, and she had no idea where he was going. 'Like how?' And then as he paused as if he wasn't sure how to answer, she decided this was deeply scary and a girl had to set some limits.

'Can we get some ground rules in place?' she ventured, searching wildly for some way to ground herself. Employment as a palace nanny... What did she know of such a job? What did royal nannies do?

In the absence of a job description, maybe she ought to list her own.

'Ground rules?' he asked, quirking one eyebrow. Again he seemed to be on the verge of laughter, and the sensation made her feel crazy.

'No washing, no ironing and definitely no scrubbing the stairs on hands and knees,' she said wildly, while he and Zoe looked on with astonishment. 'No attending royal banquets and sitting at the bottom of the table where I don't know anyone. Neither will I wear a calf-length uniform with a starched collar and *Nanny* embroidered on the front. Nor will I curtsey or walk out of Zoe's presence backwards. No shoe shining, no...'

'But we do still need to go,' Zoe said, cutting into a tirade that was getting...well, more than a bit irrational.

Elsa paused. She looked at Stefanos's hiked eyebrows— both of them were hiked now. His lips were twitching.

Maybe she was being just ever so slightly over the top.

She struggled for calm. Hysteria wasn't what was needed, she told herself severely. Nor was treating this as a crazy joke. She needed to stay practical and focus on Zoe—regardless of whether or not Stefanos was laughing at her.

In her short life Zoe had faced her parents' deaths, and then more hospitals and doctors and paramedics and social workers than Elsa wanted to think about. Almost all of them talked over her head. It made Zoe mad, but usually she became quiet and passive.

Not now. She'd been listening to Elsa in astonishment, but with an attention more suitable to one twice her age. Now she turned to Stefanos and frowned.

'Elsa doesn't have to do all that stuff, does she?'

'No,' Stefanos said definitely. 'I think Elsa's been reading too many fairy tales.'

'But there really is a palace?'

'There really is a palace,' he said and smiled at her. 'And you really are a princess.'

He'd hooked Zoe, Elsa thought frantically. Just because he had a smile to die for.

Just because he was logical, thoughtful and he sounded as if he cared. Just because he was smiling at Zoe now with kindness and also the trace of a challenge, convincing her that this could be some sort of magical adventure.

He was glancing at her with a quizzical look that was kind as well as knowing.

How could he be kind? What did she know of the man?

What did she know about the island?

'What…what medical facilities are on the island?' she managed, trying valiantly to sound grown-up, sensible and in control. Or at least as grown-up, sensible and in control as Zoe.

'Zoe will have me to care for her,' he told her, matching her tone. 'And there's specialist backup in Athens.'

'There are no paediatricians on Khryseis?'

He hesitated. 'Education has hardly been King Giorgos's concern,' he admitted at last. 'In fact he's actively discouraged it. Even I haven't been able to work there. Giorgos wouldn't permit me to practice medicine on Khryseis, so I've built my career elsewhere.'

'There are no medical facilities at all?' she asked incredulously.

'There's one elderly doctor and a midwife. Up until now the fishermen have taken really ill islanders to Athens.'

'You're kidding me.'

'Sadly, no.'

'And…and now?'

'And now we go back to the island and think about the future from there.'

'You'll get more medical staff?'

'That's one of my first priorities. The island's not big enough to support a huge range of specialties but there will be good basic medicine with fast transfers to Athens at need.'

He hesitated. 'Elsa, you will be looked after,' he said, gently but strongly. 'You both will. So no, Elsa, you will not be asked to scrub stairs or polish silver. You'll be on the island as Zoe's friend and as her nanny, for as long as you wish to stay. I'll ask nothing more of you. This isn't a trap, Elsa. I promise you. No strings.' His face broke into another of his magical smiles. 'Our island's lovely, Elsa. Zoe. We can work things out. The three of us. Please?'

His smile caught her and held. Demanding a response. How could she resist an appeal like this?

And, despite her fears, a tiny trickle of excitement crept in.

She had no idea where this man was coming from—or where he was going—but his smile was mesmerising. And as well as that…

She and Zoe had eaten sandwiches for lunch almost every day for four years. She'd had to chop wood to cook and to heat their water. Wood-chopping jarred her hip so much that sometimes it was hard not to just give in. But there was never the choice of giving in.

But now…Stefanos was offering them a home in a palace on an island in the Mediterranean. He was offering her a well-paid job. She'd have no more money worries. No wood-chopping. Did he realise how enticing it sounded? This man might appear seriously sexy but right now it was the lack of wood-chopping that was more seductive.

'I do need to keep my research skills up,' she muttered, fighting to sound practical and reserved and wary.

'Of course. I see you doing the same things you're doing now. With Zoe.'

'Home-schooling?'

'We can get a tutor. Zoe, you'll need to learn Greek.'

'I already know Greek,' Zoe said proudly.

'You already know...'

'Christos spoke Greek to her as a baby,' Elsa told him, feeling a bit smug herself as she noted his astonishment. 'We figured it was part of who she was, so we've kept it up.'

'Elsa speaks it now too,' Zoe added, 'and we both read it. There are two old Greek ladies in Waratah Cove. We visit them once a week and talk with them, and Elsa does their shopping and says it's payment for our lessons. If we went away I'd miss them.' Her face clouded. 'And the cats. How can we go away without our cats?'

'Yeah, the cats,' Elsa said, as if it was a challenge.

He grinned at that. 'That's one more thing fixed. Zoe, open the blue suitcase.'

She opened it. Fascinated. To display cat food. Bulk cat food. A suitcase of cat food.

'So we're supposed to open the suitcase and come home when they need a refill?' Elsa said and she couldn't help sounding waspish.

'That's fixed too,' he said, his grin teasing her to smile with him. 'There's a guy who works round here tending gardens, doing odd jobs. I've arranged for him to visit every night at dusk, feed the cats, lock them up, then let them out at dawn. In perpetuity. And if any other stray comes along then he's to do exactly what you'd do. Take it in, get it neutered, tell it the house rules. He can even do your two Greek ladies' shopping if you want. Now... Any more objections?'

'My...my house?' Elsa stammered.

'I told you, he does gardens and odd jobs. He'll maintain this place as long as we want.'

'You found this guy when?'

'The concierge at the hotel earned his keep last night,' he said, and grinned again. 'He brought his wife in to help. His wife knows you and knows what you need. So there you go. Local knowledge and my cash.'

'Yeah, your cash,' she said, breathless. 'We can't take it.'

'See, what you don't understand is that you can,' he said. 'Zoe's a princess. You're nanny to a princess. Are there any other problems?'

'The medical facilities...'

'I'll be there and, as I said, there are fast flights to Athens. Until we get other medical facilities organised we can cope.' He took her hand again and held, and with his other hand he took Zoe's. 'Khryseis needs a team,' he said. 'A royal team. Prince Regent, Princess Zoe and Nanny Elsa. Do we have it?'

'Yes,' Zoe said.

There were no arguments left. The only one that was still swirling round and round in her mind was, I don't want to be a nanny to your prince.

But that was dumb. She glanced at the mantel where Matt still smiled.

Definitely it was dumb.

He glanced to where she'd looked. Saw what she'd been looking at.

Didn't ask a question.

'It'll be fine,' he said softly, and the pressure on her hand strengthened. Then, before she knew what he was about, he put his hand under her chin and tilted it—and kissed her. It was a feather-light kiss, quickly over, and why it had the capacity to make her feel...make her feel...

No. She had to stop thinking about how it made her feel, because that was nonsense. But his hand was still under her chin, forcing her to meet his gaze.

'I will keep you safe,' he said, strongly and surely. 'And Zoe too. You've worked too hard for too long, Elsa Murdoch. Now it's up to Zoe and me to see you have some fun. Just say yes.'

And what else was she to do?

'I guess...yes,' she managed, but she didn't add, Yes, Your Royal Highness. Because that would be agreeing to all of it. The whole royal fairy tale.

Ridiculous.

CHAPTER SIX

Two weeks later they left Australia, luxuriating in first class seats on a direct flight to Athens, to be followed by a smaller plane to Khryseis.

'I'll be on Khryseis to meet you,' Stefanos had said in one of the scores of calls he'd made since then. 'But our people will take care of you all the way.'

They hadn't seen him since that fateful lunch. He'd had to leave. 'Things are chaotic,' he'd said. 'I need to get back to the island straight away but I promise I won't let that disorder touch you.'

It wasn't touching them now. They were in first class airline seats. They had a cocoon each, with every conceivable gadget, including one that turned the seats into beds at the flick of a switch. A hostess had already made Zoe's bed for her, with crisp linen and fluffy duvet, and she was fast asleep.

Elsa was staring out of the window and seeing what was probably Hawaii.

She was trying not to gibber.

She'd been on one overseas flight in her life. To Tasmania. She didn't remember all that many gadgets and duvets and cocoons on that flight. She remembered being served a packet of nuts and a warm beer.

She was about to be a nanny to a princess.

The princess was bone weary. Her little body still wasn't up to strength. The last weeks had been excitement plus, and Elsa had worried about the wisdom of letting her go at all.

'But it's imperative,' Stefanos had said in his deep, grave voice and, dumb or not, she believed him. If Zoe wasn't there he had no power to replace the council. He had no power to stop the corruption he told her was endemic.

So, once again, why rail against something she had no control over? Now, as Zoe snuggled into sleep, she thought with this level of luxury maybe her little charge could enjoy herself.

Maybe *she* could enjoy herself.

Amazingly, her hip wasn't hurting. Normally, sitting for more than a couple of hours made it ache unbearably, but her hip obviously decided it liked first class treatment, thank you very much, and it wasn't only her hip thinking it.

She was on her way to live in a castle. As a nanny. A nanny, she reminded herself. A paid servant. She'd get to eat in the servants' quarters, while Zoe ate in state. She'd use chipped pottery while Zoe swanned round in party dresses, using cut-glass crystal and silverware, attended by butlers and...and whatever else royalty had.

Um...this was Zoe she was talking about. Maybe she couldn't see that happening.

And tucked in her bag was a document, prepared by Stefanos's legal team, read from all angles by her local lawyer and then faxed to a team of international lawyers in Canberra for a final check.

The document said that if, at any time, Zoe seemed so distressed that it was damaging her mental or physical health—and that decision was to be made by a team of independent *Australian* medical experts flown out at Stefanos's expense—then Zoe's fare back to Australia would be paid immediately. And so would hers.

So. Maybe it'd work?

But...she was a marine biologist, not a nanny.

Stefanos had promised her starfish.

Yeah, great. She shoved that thought as far back in her head as she could. She'd like to be rid of it completely—the ache to follow her own dreams.

But Zoe came first. Zoe was more important than dreams. And maybe those dreams could still be resurrected. If Zoe was unhappy they'd come home.

Catch-22. She didn't want Zoe to be unhappy.

'But we can make it a game,' she'd whispered to Zoe as she'd watched her little charge drift towards sleep. 'You being a princess in a castle.'

'With a prince,' Zoe had said sleepily. 'Isn't he nice?'

He is nice, Elsa admitted. Um…all things considered, he's very nice.

Which was why she had to remember that he was a prince and she was a nanny. A nanny with a sliver of a career left as a marine biologist, who could maybe be happy with starfish.

Certainly a nanny with no interest whatsoever in a prince. Even if he was as drop-dead gorgeous as Stefanos.

Especially if he was as drop-dead gorgeous as Stefanos!

She closed her eyes. Two seconds later the hostess was beside her. 'Can I make your bed up for you, ma'am? Here are your pyjamas.'

She handed her a pair of pink silk pyjamas.

There was a well-known Australian politician sitting in the seat diagonally in front of her—she recognised him from the newspapers. He was wearing blue silk pyjamas as he read the financial pages.

What a shame Stefanos wasn't with them, she thought. He'd look really cute in blue pyjamas.

See, she told herself sternly. That's what nannies are paid not to think.

What are nannies paid to think?

Not about lost careers. Not about lost dreams.

And not about drop-dead gorgeous Prince Regents.

Stefanos paced the palace balcony and waited for them, feeling ridiculous. The staff were beside themselves with excitement, so much so that he'd given in and done the dress-up thing again. He'd done it twice now, once in Australia at the formal reception and again today. Hopefully there wouldn't be too many more occasions where he had to feel so ridiculous.

But maybe there would be.

This whole situation was crazy, he told himself, for maybe the thousandth time since he'd heard the news of Christos's death. He was automatically Prince Regent—island ruler until Zoe turned twenty-five—but, although the Regency gave him some powers, the thing he wanted most was denied to him.

He wanted the island to be a democracy, but as Regent he had no power to change the constitution. Democracy would have to wait for Zoe to turn twenty-five.

Since he was a kid he'd dreamed of Khryseis being a great and wonderful place to live. But now...he'd fallen in love with his medicine. He was good at his job. His research was vitally important, and he loved what he did.

What could he do here but tinker round the edges, protect the islanders from the worst of the excesses they'd endured in the past, then—what?—try and remember his general medicine so he could treat the islanders' minor ailments until Zoe came of age? In what, seventeen years?

Then he'd go tamely back to the States and pick up where he'd left off? To a career that was waiting for him?

Yeah, and pigs would fly.

He had no choice. He had to care for the island. He had to care for Zoe.

And Elsa?

She needed care as much as Zoe, he thought. Elsa had stood up to him with the air of a battered warrior, a woman accustomed to having her world shift and accepting those shifts with as much dignity and grace as she could muster. He'd seen how much the thought of losing Zoe terrified her, but once she'd realised how needful it was she'd simply got on with it.

He had the feeling that even if he hadn't offered her a generous salary, she'd still be doing exactly what she was doing. Taking care of Zoe, no matter what life threw at her.

What had life thrown at her?

He needed to find out more about her—and her husband. Why was he no longer on the scene? She still wore a wedding ring.

Um…why was that relevant?

He should have found out. His enquiries had been professional. It had seemed wrong to pry.

But he wanted to know.

He did already know some things. For one… *She seemed loving.* For some dumb reason that phrase had been playing in his head since he'd met her. Her fierce devotion to Zoe was touching something in him that he'd learned to ignore a long time ago.

He didn't do emotion. Since he'd left this island as a teenager he'd been totally committed to his medicine. Yet here he was, not only realising he'd have to abandon the work he was passionate about but, in the stillness of the night, as he lay trying to find a way he could sort all his commitments, Alexandros's idle teasing kept rising up to taunt him.

Wife. Family.

No!

He remembered the horror of his father's death, and his mother's anguish as she'd insisted he take a scholarship to the US to keep him safe. He remembered grief and homesickness, and his mother's death had cemented his knowledge that love caused nothing but pain. Work had been his salvation then, as it could be his salvation now—whether or not it was the work he desperately wanted to do.

'If you please…' A delicate cough sounded behind him and he jumped a foot. The old palace butler moved like a cat. One of these days the old guy was going to give him a heart attack.

He turned and tried to look as if he hadn't had a fright. 'Yes?'

'I believe they've arrived, sir,' the old man said gravely.

He glanced out at the magnificent formal driveway. An ancient Rolls-Royce was proceeding in state down the avenue, the flag of Khryseis flying proudly from the grille.

The butler was beaming with pride and anticipation. That was what this was all about, Stefanos thought grimly. Giving the islanders back their identity.

Which was why he was wearing this ridiculous uniform.

But there were other imperatives hammering at him. Back in New York he had a surgical list still waiting. He couldn't let those kids down. He'd have to return before he could finally commit himself to this place.

The car had pulled to a halt and the driver stepped out. He must be eighty as well—half the retainers in this household were in their dotage—but, like most of the staff, he was also wearing the imposing uniform of the Khryseis royal household.

Since Giorgos's death, since the islanders had discovered they could revert to their own royal family, the excitement had been building. The Isle of Sappheiros now had its own royal family in its palace. So did the Isle of Argyros. Khryseis, the smallest of the islands, was last to revert to rule by its original royal family, and the islanders were looking to Stefanos to make this good.

And they were also looking to this one little girl, coming home. A child who must be protected.

At least he could share that responsibility, he thought, once more feeling grateful for Elsa. Ruling the island might be his duty but with Elsa here he didn't need to commit emotionally. If he kept Zoe safe and her nanny happy, then that was the extent of his obligations.

The Crown Princess was loved by a woman called Elsa. Which meant the love bit could be shelved as not his business.

Elsa and Zoe climbed from the Rolls-Royce and if they weren't quite clutching each other they came awfully close.

'This is really scary,' Zoe whispered, and Elsa couldn't agree more.

It was a palace. A real, honest to goodness palace, vast and ancient. Turrets, battlements, spires and flags, vast entrance steps and Grecian columns, all set against a magical backdrop—sapphire seas, golden beaches, white cliffs with mountains in the background.

Internet pages they'd read had told them that Khryseis was the most impoverished of the three Diamond Isles, but once it had been fabulously wealthy. This palace backed it up. Elsa had never seen a building so fantastic. Or big.

'I hope we don't have to dust and hoover it,' she whispered to Zoe, and Zoe giggled. The tension eased.

Only then Stefanos strode out of the vast front entrance and the tension zoomed back again.

'Ooo er…' Elsa muttered, and Zoe clutched her hand and gave another shaky giggle. Striding down the great granite steps towards them, Stefanos looked like something out of history. Romantic history.

'He's a real prince again. Do you think he wears a sword?' Zoe whispered, awed.

'Hey, he is,' Elsa said as he got closer and they could see the great golden hilt emerging from its scabbard. 'Be good, Zoe.'

'It's only Stefanos. He won't hurt us,' Zoe said, and it was the child who was trying to reassure the adult.

Some nanny she made, Elsa thought. Telling her charge to be scared.

Actually, she wasn't a great nanny at all. She looked down at her scuffed trainers—she'd needed comfy shoes for the flight and these were all she had. For the last four years she'd lived in jeans and sweatshirts. If her royal duties demanded better clothes, they'd need to wait until pay day.

Zoe, however, looked beautiful. In her sparkly new clothes, her dark curls held back with diamanté butterfly clips, her pretty blue sandals adorned with butterflies, she looked every inch a child of royalty.

Underneath her carefully chosen clothes were scars which were still healing, but her new clothes hid them and gave her confidence. As this man coming towards them was giving her excitement.

'I'm going to be a princess,' she whispered.

'And I'm going to be a nanny,' Elsa whispered back.

'Stefanos said we could still look for starfish,' the child said, picking up on her nerves and, amazingly, trying to reassure her.

'He did, didn't he,' Elsa said and fought for a bit more backbone—the courage to pin a cheerful smile in place and turn to greet her employer.

What in the world was she doing here? And why did the sight of the man strolling towards her make her knees feel as if they were turning to jelly?

'Welcome to Khryseis, Princess Zoe.' Stefanos strode towards them and he greeted Zoe first. He took her hands and stooped to kiss her cheeks. It might be a normal Greek greeting but here, now, it seemed a truly royal gesture. Zoe looked suitably amazed.

'I'm not a real princess,' she told him, as if admitting a falsehood.

'You are,' Stefanos said gently. 'Your father was the Crown Prince Christos and you're his daughter. This is where you belong.'

'It's a really big palace.'

'It is.'

'Elsa says we might have to dust and hoover,' she ventured, and Stefanos turned to Elsa and his dark eyes lit with laughter.

'Welcome to you, too,' he said and it was her turn to have her hands grasped and her cheek kissed. Was this the way royalty greeted nannies? 'I promise you no hoovering—and I'm so glad you decided to come.'

Whew. This was a formal gesture, she told herself wildly. He'd kissed her cheek and smiled at her. Why that had the capacity to make her insides melt…

She'd been isolated for too long. She was starting to feel… Like she had no business in the world feeling.

'Zoe was never coming alone,' she managed.

'No,' he said, but something in his tone said that such a

concept wasn't unthinkable. 'She'll be so much happier with you.'

'She…she will.' It was really hard to breathe while he was smiling at her—while he was so close—but she had to start as she meant to go on. 'And thank you for making us feel right at home, by the way.'

'Sorry?'

'By wearing your casual gear,' she said, and managed to smile. 'It makes me feel I'll fit right in.'

His eyes met hers, laughter meeting laughter. But he couldn't respond how he wished. He was aware their conversation was being listened to, even if she wasn't.

There were only three staff members within sight, but every window was open and the palace curtains were inched back enough to allow the servants to hear. He'd deliberately not lined the staff up to meet Zoe, but the islanders' desperate need for a new royal family had to be met.

'Would you like to see your bedrooms?' he asked them both.

'Um…bedrooms,' Elsa said. 'Plural?'

'I want to stay with Elsa,' Zoe said urgently and Stefanos smiled a reassurance.

'I don't blame you. Come and see what we've organised. You'll need to meet a couple of people first. The housekeeper. The butler. We'll leave the rest of the staff for you to meet tomorrow.'

'Oh, goody,' Elsa whispered, and Stefanos smiled in sympathy.

'There's a photo shoot here after lunch,' he added apologetically. 'Christos was well loved on the island and there's huge interest and pleasure that his child is coming home. To ban all photographers would have had cameramen scaling walls, so I've permitted a representative from each of the island's media outlets.'

'You have more than one?' Elsa said, incredulous.

'It's not a complete backwater,' he said gently and she flushed.

'You have multi-media outlets and you have only one doctor?'

'I know—priorities that need fixing. They will be fixed, but I haven't managed everything in two weeks.' He took Zoe's hand and grinned down at her encouragingly. 'You want to see your bedroom? You have a four-poster bed with curtains.'

'Yes, please,' Zoe said breathlessly. She turned with him and they headed up the grand entrance steps.

Leaving Elsa to follow.

I'm the nanny, she told herself, trying not to feel bereft and hopelessly out of her comfort zone. Staying in the background is what I'm supposed to do.

Stefanos and Zoe reached the top step and paused, looking back to her.

They looked fabulous, she thought. Prince Regent and his Crown Princess. Zoe looked lit up like a fairy on top of a Christmas tree, holding her big cousin's hand with confidence.

'Are you coming?' Stefanos said gently. She met his gaze and realised that once again he'd guessed how she was feeling.

Zoe still needed her, she thought wildly. She wasn't being put out to pasture yet.

'I'm coming,' she called. The chauffeur was lifting their bags out of the boot and she grabbed the top one. The heaviest.

'Leave that to the staff,' Stefanos told her.

'I'm the staff,' she said determinedly and, to her amazement, he chuckled.

'I don't think so,' he said. 'I expect the staff to conform to a certain standard in their uniform. I need to tell you that your standard falls a long way short until we can get you outfitted as befits your status…as a friend of the Crown Princess.'

Then his tone became gentle and the laughter faded. 'You've worked hard already,' he said, looking down at her from the top step, and he spoke loudly and clearly enough for his voice to carry into all those open windows. 'You've cared for my little cousin—for our Crown Princess—with all the love at your disposal. It would be my honour to grant you a holiday for as long as you want. Your nominal title is nanny to Zoe, but my command to you personally—to you both— is to have fun.'

CHAPTER SEVEN

THEIR apartments were stunning—two apartments with an adjoining door. Rooms almost big enough to house a tennis court.

'They're built for the Crown Prince and Crown Princess,' Stefanos told them while Zoe and Elsa stared in incredulity.

'This is something out of a museum,' Elsa murmured. 'You know the ones I mean? This is the bed where Charles the First spent the night before the Great Wiggery Foppery of Seventeen Sixty-Two.'

'The Great Wiggery Foppery?' Stefanos asked, bemused.

'Or maybe it was the Great Gunfire Pirouette with Catherine Wheels,' she told him, desperately striving for humour in the face of splendour that was just plain intimidating. 'I'm Australian so my knowledge of royalty is distinctly hazy, but my grandma had a book on Bedrooms of the World. I read it when I was seven and I had chickenpox. They all had descriptions like Queen Anne had dropsy in this very bed and threw up on this very pillow. And no, don't ask me what dropsy is.'

'Are we really going to sleep in here?' While Elsa was covering her nerves with nonsense, Zoe was awed into hushed delight.

'They've changed the sheets since the great dropsy plague,' Stefanos said gravely. 'I think it might be safe to sleep in them again.'

Zoe giggled.

Which was the whole point of the exercise, Elsa reminded herself. If she could keep Zoe giggling…

But for how long?

'We'll sleep in this one,' Zoe said, and proceeded to clamber up onto what was surely intended as the Crown Prince's bed. It was vast, with four golden posts, a golden canopy and rich burgundy curtains drawn back with gold tassels.

'Then Elsa will sleep in the other one,' Stefanos said, motioning through the open door to a bedroom almost as large and a bed almost as luxurious.

The giggling stopped. Zoe's bottom lip trembled.

'No,' she said. 'This is too big by myself. We sleep in the same room at home. Why can't we sleep in the same room here?'

'We can,' Elsa said. 'There's no need to worry Prince Stefanos, though. We'll fix it.'

'You've been sharing a room with Zoe?' Stefanos asked.

'I have.' She met his gaze with open defiance.

'So you had only one bedroom in that little cottage?'

'Zoe has nightmares,' she said. 'Even if we had ten bed-rooms we wouldn't use them.'

'I'm not sure the staff will approve of a trundle bed in here. They're wanting Zoe to be real royalty.'

'So Zoe gets the four-poster and I get a trundle.'

'There needs to be some delineation.'

'I'm her friend and her guardian.'

'Yes, and her nanny.'

'So I am,' she said, figuring that here was a line in the sand—her first test. Zoe would not be made to suffer from the demands of royalty. 'So it's back to the trundle. Zoe will not sleep alone.'

'I don't like alone,' Zoe said, relaxing now she was sure Elsa was on her side.

'We'll sort it out,' Stefanos went on in a voice that said this issue wouldn't go away.

'If you think…'

'Leave it,' he said, and she met his gaze head-on. 'Zoe, take a look at the beach.'

Zoe looked—while Elsa met Stefanos's gaze and held. He smiled at her and she thought, Don't you dare. You smile at me and you think you can get away with murder.

The scary thing was that she suspected he could.

'Look at the beach, Elsa,' he said gently, and she tore her gaze away from his and looked.

The palace gardens led down to a wide stretch of golden sand, a cove of shallow water and low, rolling waves.

'Wow,' Zoe breathed. 'Can we swim?'

'As soon as you're settled.' He hesitated, watching Elsa. Who forced her thoughts back to beds.

If he thought he could get his own way simply by smiling… She took a deep breath and started to form a cogent argument about trundle beds, but he'd moved on.

'Lunch is in half an hour,' he told them. 'We'll organise the beds later. Meanwhile, I'll leave you to get settled. The butler will let you know when lunch is ready, and he'll show you the way.'

'Can't we just come down in half an hour?' Elsa asked.

'You'd get lost,' he told her and there was that smile again. 'And now we have you both here we don't intend to lose you. Make yourselves at home and I'll see you at lunch.'

He went out. Elsa was left with confusion, an unaccountable fear and the knowledge that the room was bleaker for his going.

What was it about the man? In his presence she felt about the same age as Zoe.

This was crazy. It was just his uniform, she told herself. The fairy tale bit. He looked so…royal.

'Stefanos said we're getting our photos taken after lunch,' Zoe ventured, looking worried. 'Should I wear something pretty?'

'You look very pretty right now,' she said and gave the little girl a swift hug. A hug she needed just as much as Zoe. 'But maybe we can find you something even prettier. What about your new dress?'

They came down to lunch looking nervous. Zoe was wide-eyed with wonder, clutching Elsa's hand as if it were a lifeline—but she wasn't subdued, Stefanos thought, as he watched them walk down the stairs towards him. She looked like a little girl about to go to a birthday party where she didn't know anyone. It was a bit scary, but it might turn out to be fun.

Elsa, on the other hand, looked nervous in a different way. It was as if she was nervous of her royal surroundings. More. She was nervous of him?

She was still wearing jeans and sweatshirt. Zoe was in the most extravagant of the clothes he'd bought for her—her beautiful party dress. Beside her, Elsa looked subdued. She looked even more subdued when she saw him waiting for them at the foot of the stairs. It was this uniform, he thought regretfully. It was enough to scare *him*. After the media call he could take it off, but until then he had to be a prince.

So. He was a prince. Zoe was a princess. Elsa looked as if she didn't want to be here at all.

And she was still limping. He hadn't noticed when she'd arrived, but watching her coming down the stairs he saw it again. She was holding the balustrade with her spare hand and doing her best to disguise it, but she was being careful. The way she swung her left leg forward... There wasn't full movement in her hip and it looked as if coming downstairs hurt.

Last time he'd seen her he'd seen the faintest trace of a limp. She'd brushed it aside when he'd enquired, and he'd had so much on his mind then that to assume it was a temporary sprain had been the easiest option. Now, though... There was a lot he had to find out about this woman.

Like what was the damage with her leg.

Like why she was coming to lunch and a media call in faded

jeans and sweatshirt. Looking scared. Up until now he would have described her as spirited and feisty. What was it about this place that was sucking the spirited and feisty out of her?

He glanced up at the massive chandelier above his head—two thousand crystals, the housekeeper had told him, and he didn't doubt it for a minute—and he thought, What's oppressive about this?

He smiled at them and Zoe let go of Elsa's hand and bounced down the last few steps to greet him. She gazed up at the chandelier and breathed deeply in small girl satisfaction.

'It's really, really beautiful,' she said.

'So are you,' he told her and she giggled.

He glanced at Elsa—and caught her unawares. There was a wash of pure, unmitigated pain on her face. It was gone as soon as it had come, quickly turned into a smile, but he knew he wasn't mistaken.

'We're hungry,' she said, a trifle too fast, and he thought she was still in defence mode.

'Excellent,' he said. 'In fact, more than excellent when you see what's in front of us.'

He led the way into the dining room and paused at the door, smiling down to Zoe again. 'This is a welcome lunch for you,' he said gently. 'Specially made by everyone who works here.'

And it was—a feast that promised a small girl's heaven. The delicate finger food looked as if it had been designed to tempt and tantalise a little girl's appetite. There were tiny cheesy biscuits in the shape of animals. Finger-sized sausage rolls. Chicken wings with tiny chef-hat wrappers around their tips so a small hand wouldn't get greasy. Strawberries and grapes and slivers of watermelon. Tiny chocolate cakes with a dusting of sugar. Miniature sponge cakes with the tops turned into wings and fixed in place with a mix of red jelly and cream. Petite eclairs with creamy custard filling.

Around them the room was a mass of fresh cut flowers, a wondrous fantasy feast of beauty and pure delight.

Zoe sat down and gazed at the table in awe. 'Elsa won't have to tell me to eat here,' she breathed.

'That's what we hoped,' he said and glanced at Elsa again—and got that look again. Raw pain.

'You don't approve?' he asked and she caught herself and managed to smile. But her smile was strained. She was having trouble disguising how hard it was to summon it at all.

'It's wonderful,' she said.

'So why do you look unhappy?' he asked gently.

'Elsa's a bit sad 'cause she hasn't got any pretty clothes,' Zoe said and popped a strawberry into her mouth—and then looked mortified. She swallowed it manfully and looked even more guilty. 'Is…is it okay to start?'

'Absolutely it's okay to start,' Stefanos said and handed over the sausage rolls. Zoe took two—and then looked at how small they were and took another.

'Thank you very much,' she breathed, and Stefanos glanced at the door. He knew at least six members of staff were behind there, holding their breath that she'd like their offering, that she'd be a kind child, that she could be a princess to be proud of.

She was all of those things, he thought. And it was thanks to Elsa.

Elsa, who didn't have pretty things to wear.

'So you don't have any dresses?' he probed and she cast him a glance that was almost resentful.

'I didn't bring any. And I'm not sad because of that. It's just…I'm just a bit overwhelmed.'

'You mean yesterday there was just you loving Zoe,' he said gently. 'And now there's me and a palace full of staff and an island ready to love her.'

'It's crazy to think like that,' she said, but she did.

'So back to the clothes,' he said gently. 'Can I ask why there's nothing but jeans?'

'I'm a marine biologist. Why would I need dresses?'

There was a loaded silence. Zoe ate two sausage rolls and

a strawberry and then thought about what Elsa had said. And decided she might add her pennyworth.

'Elsa did have pretty clothes,' the child told him, considering an eclair. 'Only she got too skinny and they looked funny on her. We kept them for ages but then she said, "You know what, Zoe, I'm never going to be this size again; they might as well make someone else happy." So we packed them up and took them to a church fair. And Mrs Henniker bought Elsa's prettiest yellow dress and she looked awful in it and Elsa cried.'

'I did not,' Elsa said, fighting for dignity. 'I had hay fever.'

'You only get hay fever when you cry,' Zoe said wisely. 'Giving your clothes away made you really sad.'

The bond between these two was amazing. Up until now he'd thought it was Elsa who did all the giving. Suddenly a new view was opening up.

Zoe was eight going on thirty.

Elsa was…sometimes ninety. Sometimes a kid.

She was trying for indignant here but it wasn't coming off. Zoe had exposed her and she knew she was exposed.

'Why did you lose weight?'

'I stopped eating for a while,' she told him in a voice that said no more questions were welcome. 'I've started again.'

'We might need to buy you some clothes,' he said, and watched as vulnerability disappeared, to be replaced by indignation.

'You don't need to buy me anything. I like my jeans.'

'I like your jeans too,' he said—and he did. They were exceedingly cute. Mind, she could do with a bit more flesh on her frame. She was almost elfin. And that limp…

'What happened to your leg?' he asked, and got another scared look.

'Please…just leave it. I'm here to be with Zoe while she gets to know the country her papa came from. I intend to stay in the background. Can we leave it at that?'

He considered her gravely and shook his head. 'Zoe, what's wrong with Elsa's leg?'

He heard her gasp. He didn't look at her.

This woman had cared for Zoe for four years. If he'd known of Christos's death he would have been there for his little cousin. The responsibility was his, but he hadn't even known of Zoe's existence.

That hurt on all sorts of levels, and one of those levels was the fact that this woman seemed to have put her life on hold for Zoe—and it might be worse than that.

He'd watched her come down the stairs and realised this was no twisted ankle. She was protecting her hip—as she'd been protecting her hip two weeks ago on the beach but he'd been too preoccupied to see it.

'She hurt it when my mama and papa died,' Zoe said, not picking up on the undercurrents. She was back considering food. This meal was a huge success. He could practically hear the chef's sigh of happiness from here.

'Are you going to tell me how badly?' he asked Elsa.

'I broke my hip,' she said discouragingly.

'You were in the car accident with Zoe's parents?'

'Yes.'

'And your husband…' He hadn't put two and two together, but he did now, and he didn't like it.

'Elsa's Matty was killed too,' Zoe said, and she was suddenly grave and mature and factual. 'My mama and papa were in the front seat and Matty and Elsa and me were in the back. A great big truck came round the corner on the wrong side of the road and hit our camper van and our camper van started to burn. Elsa pulled me out but she couldn't pull anyone else out. We were both really, really sad. I was in hospital for a long time—I can hardly remember—but I do remember Elsa coming in a wheelchair to see me. She says my grandma came to see me too, but I can't remember that. I remember being in a bath a lot and crying, but Elsa was always there. And then my grandma got sick so Elsa took me home with her—and now we're living happily ever after.'

She was suddenly back to being a little girl again. Happy

and optimistic. 'Only this is a better place for happy ever after, isn't it, Elsa?'

'There was nothing wrong with my beach,' Elsa said, making an unsuccessful attempt to glower, and Zoe giggled as if she'd said something silly.

'No, but our beach doesn't have cream puffs. These are really good. Can I have another one, please?'

'Be my guest,' Stefanos said and he handed her the plate—but his eyes were on Elsa. 'So why are you still limping?'

And once again it was Zoe who answered. 'Mr Roberts says she should have another operation. Mr Roberts came to see Elsa last time I was in hospital and he said, "When are we going to fix that hip, young lady?" And Elsa said, "When I have the time and the money, and like that's going to happen soon." And Mr Roberts said she had to get her pi…her priorities right and she said she did.'

'Zoe, don't,' Elsa said, looking desperate. 'Please, sweetheart, this is nothing to do with Prince Stefanos.'

'No, but he's nice,' Zoe said, as if that excused everything. 'Can I have one of those cakey things with wings, please?'

What would happen if she just got up from the table, walked right out of here, straight to the ferry, then on a plane back to Australia?

She had a return ticket. That was one of her stipulations about coming.

It was a first class ticket. If she traded it for economy she'd have enough to live on until she could start back to work.

Zoe didn't need her.

Only of course Zoe did. She looked happy and contented but she'd been here for less than a day. She was still clutching her. She was happy because this was exciting and Stefanos was kind. And the rest. Big and too good-looking for his own good—and did he know how sexy he looked in that uniform?

He was doing her head in and her head had to stay intact. She had to stay practical. She needed to find a role for herself here that wasn't tied to Zoe or Stefanos or the palace.

She could do this, she thought. She just had to stay detached from Stefanos and his dangerous charm.

This man was important to her only in his relationship to Zoe. He was good to Zoe. He made the little girl laugh. But he hadn't gained so much trust that Elsa could walk away.

She didn't ever want to walk away. Not from Zoe. The thought hurt on so many levels that the pain in her hip didn't even register in comparison.

'What are you thinking?' Stefanos asked, watching her quizzically from the head of the table. 'To make you look like that?'

'I…nothing.'

'I don't think I've been appropriately sympathetic.'

'I don't know what appropriate sympathy is.'

'Neither do I,' he said softly. 'But if it helped I'd find it for you.'

See, there was the whole problem. She had so much going on in her head—how to fit in here—what she was going to do with herself while Zoe settled—how she was going to make a life for herself after Zoe stopped needing her, as stop she surely would—and across it all was Stefanos's gorgeous smile, the way his dark eyes creased at the corners, the way he seemed to read her mind…

He left them for a while as she drank coffee. Urgent royal business, he said and that made her even more nervous. By the time he returned she was climbing the walls.

'You don't need me for this,' she said and pushed her chair back. 'Zoe, are you okay to do this photo thing with…with your cousin? I'll go up to the bedroom and unpack.'

'No!' Zoe was out of her chair in a flash, darting round the table to grab her hand. 'You have to come with me.'

Not so settled, then. Neither would she be, she thought, if someone told her she had to meet the press.

'I've arranged for Elsa to come with us,' Stefanos told Zoe, and her heart hit her boots.

'Excuse me?'

'I've promised the press they can meet Zoe and you.'

'And me?'

'You're the woman who's been caring for our Crown Princess for the past four years,' he said steadily. 'The islanders would have taken Zoe to them in a heartbeat. All of us owe you a debt that touches our honour.'

He rose and held out a hand to Zoe, and the little girl hesitated for a moment and then gave him hers. It was that sort of gesture. Strong, sure, commanding. Royal.

'If Zoe's brave enough to have her photograph taken, surely you can,' he told her.

'Yes, but Zoe's a princess,' she said on a wail. 'Look at me. I'm not even a proper nanny.'

'You're not,' he agreed. 'You're our friend. And, as our friend…' He hesitated. 'Elsa, giving Zoe clothes seemed appropriate. For you, however, it seems almost insulting and I ask you to accept that it's not my intention to insult you. Nevertheless, I've made some fast phone calls and the owners of our two main dress shops are here already, setting out a selection of clothes. For Zoe's coronation you'll need evening wear and we can't get that here, but for now…it would please me if you could choose something more suitable than jeans and sweatshirt for your introduction to our island.'

She stared at him in stupefaction. 'You want me to buy clothes?'

'I want you to take the clothes that I will buy for you,' he said. 'This will be my pleasure.'

'To dress me?'

His eyes creased involuntarily into laughter. 'I don't think we're quite there yet.'

She stared at him, feeling a tide of colour sweep upward. 'Ex…excuse me?'

'Levity,' he murmured, obviously fighting to get back to being serious. 'You need to excuse me. But this is clothes, Elsa. No big deal.'

'I wear jeans.'

'Zoe says you don't. Not before the accident.'

'I'm a whole new me since the accident.'

'Then is it possible,' he said gently, 'that you can be a whole new you again?'

'I…'

'Please, Elsa.'

She stared down at her battered sneakers, her worn jeans. They were like her skin, she thought, yet another skin she was being asked to change.

Poverty-stricken single mother to royal childminder.

Single woman to wife. Eager student to earnest professional. Married woman to grieving widow.

Skins, skins, skins. She hardly knew who she was any more. What harm could one more change do?

'Fine,' she said.

'Your gratitude is overwhelming,' he murmured, and there it was again—that hint of laughter.

'Did you like it when they told you that you had to wear a sword?' she demanded.

'I…no.'

'Then pay me the compliment of allowing that I feel the same,' she whispered. 'Thank you very much for providing clothes. I accept and I'm grateful. It's just…I've learned from past experience that it hurts to change direction. I'm doing my best to smile while it happens but you'll need to excuse me when my smile falters.'

She chose a simple green sundress. Zoe and Stefanos chose a whole lot more. Presumably the photographers and journalists had been told to wait, for Stefanos refused to hurry and was only satisfied when he—and Zoe—had decided she had enough clothes to make her…pretty.

Pretty was a strange concept. She'd stopped worrying about her appearance four years ago. Now, dressed in a lovely light sundress, with shoestring straps and a skirt that twirled and swished as she walked, she decided there were definite upsides to shedding skins.

She felt…nice. Free. It was a novel experience, but it didn't stop her hanging back as she finally followed Stefanos and Zoe to the palace media centre.

At the door Stefanos stepped back and motioned for Elsa to precede him.

No way.

She shook her head and dropped deliberately further back, and there was no time for him to react. The door was open. Cameras were flashing and questions were flying.

Zoe cast her a panicked backward glance, but Stefanos lifted her up and held her in his arms.

It was the best thing he could do, Elsa thought. Holding her in his arms. Zoe would feel totally protected.

The press was absolutely riveted on Zoe—their princess coming home. Which left her mind free to wander where it willed.

She kind of liked the way she looked in this sundress. And her new sandals were pretty.

Clothes maketh the woman? The man?

Her eyes flew back to Stefanos. She could see why he'd decided to wear his uniform, but it was more than clothes, she thought. He looked confident, sure, in charge. He was assuming the mantle of control of this country.

He had a job to do and he'd do it.

And he held Zoe as if she was his own. His body language was totally protective, and in his arms Zoe felt brave enough to venture shy answers of her own, responses the media loved—responses Elsa knew would go straight to the heart of any islander.

The Prince and his little Princess. She watched them pose together, she watched Stefanos tease Zoe into laughter, and the weird sensations she'd been feeling since the first time she'd seen him standing on her beach were consolidating to something firm and definite and true. Her vision of Matty was fading still further—not disappearing entirely; she knew it could never do that—but fading to a place where he could be mourned without the constant piercing pain that had been with her for years.

She could be pretty. She could change her skin yet again with no betrayal of Matty.

What on earth was she thinking? Crazy, crazy, crazy.

A latecoming journalist jostled past her, nudging her out of her introspection. Hauling her back to reality.

Get back to earth fast, she told herself harshly. This is one of Zoe's fairy tales.

And maybe she ought to listen.

'And may I introduce Dr Elsa Murdoch?' Stefanos was saying, and she was suddenly being looked at by everyone in the room.

Doctor? She hadn't used that title since…

'It's Mrs…' she started but he wasn't allowing her to get a word in.

'Elsa—Dr Murdoch—was in the car crash that claimed Prince Christos's life,' Stefanos said, and his voice was gentle and full of compassion. 'Also killed were Zoe's mother, Amy, and Elsa's husband, Mathew. Zoe still bears the scars, physically as well as mentally, and so does Elsa. Elsa is a world expert on…what did you call starfish, Zoe?'

'Echinoderms,' Zoe volunteered. Stefanos was still holding her tightly and she obviously felt confident enough to answer. 'Or asteroidea,' she added with aplomb.

'That's the one,' Stefanos said encouragingly. 'So, for the last four years, Dr Murdoch and Zoe have been conducting echinoderm—or asteroidea—research while they've gradually healed from their injuries. Dr Murdoch has cared for Zoe with total love and commitment, and for that this country owes her an enormous debt of gratitude.'

'Hey,' she said, startled enough to forget nerves and reply with spirit. 'That sounds like you're about to give me a gold watch and a pension.'

'You deserve much, much more than that,' he said, smiling. 'I'm hoping Dr Murdoch can stay here,' he told the reporters.

'I'm hoping she'll be a constant presence in Zoe's life. I need to be away from the island for a few weeks between now and Christmas—there are ends I need to tie off before I can stay here permanently—but Zoe and, I hope, Elsa, will be happy here for ever.'

And her tingle of humour and enjoyment disappeared, just like that.

Whoa. What was he saying? That she and Zoe would be staying, but he was leaving?

I need to be away from the island...

He was planning on coming and going at will? *While...what had he said?...Zoe and, I hope, Elsa will be happy here for ever.*

She stayed rooted to the spot while more questions were aimed at Stefanos. Was his work still important to him? How committed to the island could he be if he was returning to the States? Exactly how much time would he stay here and would he still play a ceremonial role?

'You know I'm a neurosurgeon,' he was explaining to the press, 'but of course there's work for me to do here now, medical as well as political. However, there are commitments to be honoured in the States before I can take on a permanent role.'

This was never in the contract, she thought wildly. He was leaving?

Stefanos was fielding the final questions. He was saying he'd be here until the coronation, and then he'd return by Christmas. He was intending to get the council sorted within the week...

She was no longer listening.

He was leaving.

He'd organised her to wear a sundress, while he wore a sword. The way she was suddenly feeling...

Maybe she needed a sword as well.

CHAPTER EIGHT

THE media session had taken its toll on Zoe. Jet lag and excitement had finally caught up with her. As the last of the reporters left, the little girl almost visibly drooped.

'Come on, sweetheart, let's get you up to bed,' Elsa said as Stefanos brought Zoe back to her. She carefully didn't look at Stefanos. The things she needed to say to this man couldn't be said in front of Zoe. In fact, maybe they needed a sound-proofed room.

'I'm thinking you need a carriage, Your Highness,' Stefanos said grandly and scooped the little girl up again and carried her up the stairs.

Once again Elsa was left to follow. Her anger and bewilderment were building by the minute.

Stefanos was leaving. He was assuming she'd stay and take care of Zoe. In a place she didn't know. In a country she didn't know.

She was furious, but as she limped up the stairs after them her anger receded, leaving her flat and deflated. Like Zoe, she was so tired...

She'd been tired for years, but this was worse. Jet lag? No. It was betrayal, and betrayal hurt.

She stopped at the top stair and thought, I don't want to go on. I don't want to watch Stefanos tuck Zoe into bed and make her smile. I don't want to see Zoe seduced into this life of media attention, of shallowness, of wealth, with only me to protect her.

Royalty had destroyed Christos's childhood—he'd told her that. Stefanos had left the island as well, and he'd left for a reason. How could she possibly assess the risks royalty posed for such a vulnerable child as Zoe?

Regardless, Stefanos was obviously intending that she take on the burden of protecting Zoe. That was what he'd said. For ever?

She didn't follow him into the bedroom. She made it to the top stair and sat. If Zoe needed her, Stefanos would come back for her, she thought, but the way the little girl's eyelids were drooping as he'd carried her, she doubted if she'd notice if Elsa wasn't there. And if she went in now she might explode. That he demand she drop the threads of her life in Australia on command, and yet manipulate her so he could still do what he wanted… That he could return to his old life in Manhattan and leave her to care for Zoe in a place she didn't understand…

There were weary chuckles from the end of the corridor. Stefanos was making Zoe laugh.

Bully for Stefanos.

She felt dizzy, as well as angry and confused and all the rest of it. Her hip hurt. She put her head on her knees and folded her arms over her head. This was jet lag and more. Desolation, homesickness, betrayal. The world could go away…

Footsteps sounded down the hall, approaching her on the stair and pausing. She opened her eyes. A pair of black Hessian boots was in her field of vision.

Stefanos.

'Jet lag too, huh?' he said and he was smiling again. She knew he was smiling. She could hear his smile.

'It's not jet lag,' she said without looking up. 'It's anger and disgust and deception thrown in for good measure. Zoe's your cousin. What do you mean by abandoning her?'

'I'm not abandoning her,' he said, sounding surprised.

'You're going back to Manhattan.'

'Only for a few weeks.'

'Why didn't you tell us?'

There was a pause. And then… Amazingly, an honest answer. 'Because I thought you wouldn't come if I did.'

'How very perceptive.'

He sighed and sat down beside her. 'I'm sorry. I should have told you before, but I have an urgent surgical list to do before Christmas.'

'I had a paper on echinoderms to write up before Christmas,' she retorted. 'Believe it or not, it was important. Someone else is finishing it for me right now.'

'You're saying your echinoderms are more important than my surgical list?'

'You're saying your life is more important than my life?'

He hesitated. 'Elsa, I'm sorry. Of course I don't think that. But you don't understand.'

'So make me understand,' she flashed at him. 'Are there no other surgeons in New York?'

'I can't hand this over.'

'Why not?'

'I can't explain this while you're angry.'

'You don't have a choice,' she said wearily. 'From my point of view, you've conned me into bringing Zoe here. You've seduced the two of us, with your promise of palaces and lovely clothes and happy ever after. But what do I know of this life? How do I know Zoe is safe here? It was your assurance of safety and care that brought us here. How can you calmly say you're going away and leaving us when we've scarcely set foot in the place?'

She was staring downstairs at the massive chandelier below them. Wishing she wasn't in these clothes he'd bought her. Wishing she could wave a magic wand and be home with her beach and her starfish and even her disgusting fish-head cat food—somewhere where she knew the risks and could face them for her small charge; knowing exactly where she stood.

But it seemed that Stefanos wasn't backing down. He was hesitating over what to say to her but she could see that Manhattan was a done deal.

'Just explain,' she said wearily and for a moment she thought he wasn't going to say anything. And then he did.

'I work with overseas aid agencies,' he said slowly into the silence, as if he didn't yet know that he should admit it.

Aid agencies? What sort of aid agencies? What part of this could she believe? 'But you said you work in Manhattan.'

'I do. Patients come to me.'

'How?'

'Aid agencies send them,' he said bluntly, his tone implying he'd decided he might as well tell her and get it over with, whether she believed him or not. 'International aid agencies know what I do and they contact me at need. I intersperse these operations with my normal surgery—that way I can afford it. Mostly I treat people with head injuries from Africa. Neurological stuff. For children especially, as the brain continues to grow, scar tissue causes major problems. I work on techniques to remove the worst of the scar tissue without it reforming. I had to cancel some desperate cases when I realised I needed to find Zoe and get this place sorted. Those kids are still waiting. Now you're here, I need to go back, finish what I've promised and try to hand over my techniques to others to take them forward.'

'You cancelled…' She was staring at him in horror. 'You cancelled them for Zoe?'

'For the welfare of the whole island. If Zoe wasn't back here by the end of next week, then she'd forfeit the throne.'

She frowned, trying to keep up. 'But then you'd inherit.'

'You think I want it? I want to carry on my work.'

She swallowed. Hard. Trying to take this in. 'So… So you really are abandoning us?'

'No,' he said flatly. 'I can't. This place is a mess. Hell, Elsa, there's one doctor on the whole island and that's just the start of it. The local school only takes kids up to sixteen and then there's nothing. There's no infrastructure. The council needs replacing with good, solid people and they'll need support. How can I walk away and leave that to Zoe?'

'I haven't heard about this.'

'I keep it quiet.' He shrugged. 'My wealthy patients come to me in part because of my social position. To be honest, their fees pay for the other work I do, so I have to pander to them.'

'Honestly?'

'Honestly,' he said.

She stared at him. Said nothing. Stared at him still. Why did she believe him?

She did believe him. And if she did believe him...

She took a deep breath, summoned the words she needed and said them. 'I could help,' she said.

There was a loaded silence. He rose and stared down at her, as if she'd suddenly announced the arrival of aliens.

'You're kidding me,' he said at last.

'I don't say what I don't mean,' she said, and rose as well. 'Tell me what you need me to do and I'll do it.' She wasn't feeling very steady. She put her hand on the balustrade to support herself and suddenly Stefanos's hand was over hers.

'You can't,' he said softly.

'I can't help? How do you know I can't?' She tilted her chin. 'Sure, I don't know anything about this place, sure I was angry just then, but I'll get over it. You can teach me. If your work's so important, then I can try.'

The silence extended. She really was exhausted, she thought. If it wasn't for the balustrade and Stefanos's hand...

'Elsa, I'm starting to think there's nothing you can't do,' he said softly into the silence. 'There's no end to your generosity. Zoe's parents die and you abandon your career and take care of her. I arrive and tell you she's needed here and you upend your life and abandon your echinoderms and come with her. And now...your anger turns to an offer of help, just like that. If I said I had to leave tomorrow would you try and handle the council yourself?'

'Maybe I could,' she said and jutted her chin and he laughed, a lovely deep chuckle that had her confused. Veering towards anger again. If only she wasn't so tired.

'No, don't be angry, my lovely Elsa,' he said softly, and

he placed a finger under her chin. 'I'm not laughing at you. Indeed, I never could. But no. Your generosity is amazing. Stunning. And, if I could, maybe I'd be tempted. But the island needs a ruler who knows it. Like it or not, I was raised here. I know the islanders. I know the problems. No, I don't want to rule here. I want to practice my medicine. I won't be able to practice the medicine I want here, but that's a small sacrifice in the scheme of things. I've already started a training scheme back in New York. I just have to hope my work keeps going. If you could bear me to be away for these few weeks it will make all the difference.'

'You should have told me.'

'I should have told you,' he agreed. 'Indeed, I'm starting to think I should have told you many things.' Then, as she pulled slightly away from him, his hands came to rest on her shoulders. 'Thank you, Elsa. I can't believe your generosity, and I will keep you safe. I will keep Zoe safe.'

'I know you will.' Unaccountably, her eyes filled with tears. Dammit, she would not cry. *She would not cry.*

But he was too big and too close and too male.

Matty, she thought, but it was a faint echo of a love that was gone. Only…why did it feel as if she was betraying him now?

'You're as exhausted as Zoe,' Stefanos said softly. She shook her head and tried again to pull away from him—and staggered on the staircase.

But she didn't fall. This man had promised to keep her safe and that was just what he was doing.

'That hip…' he said, holding her steady.

'It's fine.'

'It's not fine. It's on my list to do something about. But not now. Now's for sleeping.' And, before she realised what he intended, she was lifted into his arms and he was striding down the hallway, just the same way he'd carried Zoe. As if her weight was nothing.

'Put… What do you think you're doing? Put me down.'

'In a moment,' he said, not breaking stride. 'You need to go where Zoe's going.'

She wanted to struggle. She really did. But suddenly all the struggle was sucked out of her.

His arms were strong, he was big and capable and he was carrying her like a child. For Elsa, who hadn't been treated as a child since…well, since she was one, the sensation was indescribable.

She could melt into these arms, she thought. She could let herself disappear, stop struggling, let these arms hold her for ever.

Was this what jet lag did to a girl?

He was at her bedroom, pushing open her door with his foot. The interconnecting door to Zoe's room was open and she could see through. Zoe was asleep already.

She suddenly felt inordinately proud of herself, that she was a good guardian, or nanny, or whatever she was supposed to be. She'd checked on her charge, even when she wasn't exactly in control herself.

And then she realised that Stefanos was carrying her through to Zoe's room. And she saw why.

Zoe's vast four-poster bed had been moved closer to the door. Zoe was fast asleep in it. And on the other side of her massive bed was another bed. A matching four-poster. Velvet curtains, a vast canopy, eiderdowns and cushions…

The room had been turned into a twin room, with two beds that were so ridiculously enormous that she gasped with incredulity.

'Wh…'

'I know it's a bit crowded,' Stefanos said, smiling down at her in a dumb, indulgent genie sort of way that for some weird reason had her heart doing backflips. 'You'll just have to slum it.'

Slum it…

Matching four-posters…

'I'm probably going to have to pay out on workers' insurance too,' he said morosely. 'Do you know how much these things weigh? It took eight of us to get it in here.'

'You…you…' She could hardly get it out.

'Idiot?' he suggested, laughing down at her and her heart did another backflip.

'Definitely idiot,' she said, trying for asperity and failing miserably. 'I... Thank you.' She was so far out of her comfort zone that she could hardly make her voice work but there was something else she badly needed to say. 'And...at the press conference...thank you for calling me Doctor.'

'It's what you are.'

'Not since Zoe needed me. I've been her mama since then. If I called myself Doctor, everyone thought I was medical. It just confused things.'

'So you stopped being Doctor and started being Mama. As you'd stop being on holiday and start bossing councillors if I asked it of you. You know, you're one special lady.'

'I am not.'

He grinned and lowered her onto the bed, and when he let her go she was aware of a sharp stab of loss.

'You want some painkillers for your hip?'

'It's not hurting.'

'I'm very sure it is.'

'It's fine!'

'Right, then,' he said and smiled again. She could hear his smile even when she didn't look at him. It was a smile that crept all around her, enveloping her in its sweetness. 'You want help to undress?'

'No,' she said and then, as she reran his question in her head, she found her voice. 'No! And...and don't think I'm not angry any more that you didn't tell me. I still am. It's just got to wait until morning.'

'That's my girl. What if I organise lunch tomorrow so we can talk about it?'

'I don't think...'

'I don't think you can think right now.'

He tugged an eiderdown from the foot of the bed and tucked it around her. 'You'd be more comfortable if you undress but I don't think I can help you there,' he said, his voice suddenly unsteady.

'No,' she said, and then couldn't think why she'd said it. Her voice didn't seem to belong to her.

'You'll be okay,' he said, looking down at her with all the tenderness in the world. As if he cared. As if he really cared.

'You'll be cared for here,' he said, echoing her thoughts. 'You and Zoe will be safe. We'll get that hip fixed. You can play with your starfish and live happily ever after.'

There was a lot to object to in that statement. He seemed to think he was reassuring her.

'I hate starfish,' she muttered.

'You hate starfish?'

'They don't do anything. They just blob. You move 'em and they just blob some more. I hate 'em.'

'You're studying them.'

'Doesn't mean I don't hate 'em.'

'You're done in, sweetheart.'

'I'm not done in. And I'm not your sweetheart.'

'You're not, are you? There's a complication to avoid.'

'Go away.'

'I will,' he said.

But he didn't. He stood gazing down at her and she didn't want him to go. She was half asleep, allowing images from the past—grief, pain, worry, even starfish—to be supplanted by this gorgeous Prince of the Blood.

Prince of the Blood. She wasn't actually sure what the term meant but she knew what it looked like. There was a Prince of the Blood smiling down at her right now, tucking in her eiderdown, looking gorgeous in his fabulous uniform. He was still wearing his sword!

'I love your sword,' she said.

'Don't encourage me,' he said. 'I'm starting to look in mirrors and swagger.'

'So you ought,' she whispered. 'Life should hold a little swagger.'

His smile softened. He stooped so his face was really close to hers and he placed a finger on her lips. To hush her? She didn't know and she didn't much care. It was enough that he was touching her.

It was suddenly incredibly important that he touch her.

'You've lost your swagger,' he said softly, almost as a whisper. 'Life's sucked it right out of you. Let me fix it for you.'

'I don't... You can't.' Matty, she thought desperately, but he'd faded even more. What remained was the memory of how grief felt, how loss felt, how she couldn't afford to fall...

'Elsa...' he said softly and as if in a dream she murmured back.

'Mmm.'

'Is it okay if I kiss you?'

Of course it wasn't. The idea was ridiculous.

But this wasn't real. It was a dream. And in her dream it was okay to kiss a prince. In her dream she could put her arms around his neck, link her hands and tug him downward.

In her dreams she could open her lips and wait for his lips to touch them.

In her dream he kissed her.

He kissed her.

Of all the dumb, stupid, complicating things to do, this must surely be the stupidest.

But she lay in her too-big bed, tucked under the vast eiderdown, looking up at him with eyes that were dreamy and close to sleep.

But not quite. She was watching him. She was smiling at him. And then her hands came up to hold him... He'd have to be inhuman to resist.

She was beautiful.

She was so different from any other woman in his world.

Slight and sexy, her sun-bleached curls were so fine they looked as if they'd float.

Her eyes were gorgeous in her too-thin face. A man could drown in those eyes.

She had eighteen freckles. He'd counted them when?

Maybe the first time he'd seen her. How many times had he recounted? And her lips were so kissable.

What made Elsa's lips more desirable than any other woman's?

Because they belonged to Elsa?

And because she was responding.

Amazingly, she was tugging him down to her and there was no way he could resist these lips. This mouth. This woman. He sank so he was sitting on the vast bed, and he gathered her into his arms—and he kissed her with all the tenderness in his heart.

She melted into him. What had provoked him to ask permission to kiss her? He didn't know. All he knew was that the desire had become overwhelming. And when his mouth met hers…

He'd kissed women in his time. None like this.

She was warm and tender, close to tears and close to laughter, exhausted by jet lag and by fear of losing Zoe, intimidated beyond belief by her surroundings…and yet she was courageous beyond belief and she was melting into his arms as if she belonged here. She was kissing as well as being kissed. Her lips were demanding, opening, aching for him, and taking him as well as giving herself.

She felt right.

She felt like…home. Home and heart.

There was a ridiculous thought. And, as the acknowledgement of how crazy it was hit home, other realities slammed in.

He did not need to be attracted to this woman. This woman meant family.

He did not do family.

All this flooded through his consciousness like a shock wave, breaking the passion of the kiss, causing his arms to stiffen a little, causing him to break away…

Or maybe it was Elsa who broke away. He hardly knew. All that was certain was that she was still in his arms but the kiss had ended and he felt a flood of regret so deep it threatened to overwhelm him.

And Elsa's eyes were clouding as well, distancing herself from him, her arms untwining themselves from around his neck and pushing against his chest. Pushing him away.

'What…what do you think you're doing?' she whispered and he knew her confusion was at least as great as his.

'What do we both think we're doing?' he said ruefully and looked down into her face and saw fear.

Fear? Where had that come from? Surely she couldn't be afraid of him.

He was a prince in a royal palace and she was…a royal nanny.

He stood up as if she burned, taking a swift step back from the bed. If she could think that…

But… 'You needn't worry,' she whispered. 'I'm not thinking you're about to rape and pillage. I have a scream that can be heard into the middle of next week.'

'Good for you,' he said unsteadily.

'Don't patronise me.'

'I never would.'

She closed her eyes. It was a defence, he knew, but he never doubted for a moment that she'd sleep.

He stood looking down at her for a long moment, trying to think of what to say. Trying to think of how he could take this from here.

'Go away,' she muttered again.

Go away? It was the only sensible thing to do.

Of course it was the sensible thing to do.

Go away, he repeated to himself and it was a direct order, but only he knew how much effort it cost him to turn on his heel and walk out of the door.

If Zoe hadn't been asleep in the next bed…

Maybe it was just as well she was.

CHAPTER NINE

ELSA woke and sunlight was streaming in though the massive French windows of their bedroom. The crystals from the chandelier above her head were sending glittering sparkles across the room.

Zoe was sitting on the end of her bed, fully dressed in another of the lovely outfits Stefanos had bought for her.

She was cuddling a kitten. A small grey kitten with a white nose, white paws and a tiny tip of white on the end of his tail.

'Go say hello to Elsa,' Zoe said, and put the kitten down and watched in satisfaction as the small creature walked along the coverlet, crouched down and put a paw out to tentatively touch Elsa's chin.

'What…where did he come from?' Elsa managed, doing a speedy visual check of the room in case Stefanos was lurking behind the curtains. Not that she was afraid of Stefanos. Not exactly.

But she wouldn't put it past the man to lurk.

'Stefanos gave him to me,' Zoe said with deep satisfaction. 'He said I must be missing my cats at home and he's mine to keep. His name is Buster.'

'Yours to keep…' Elsa said cautiously. This needed thinking about.

There were things like quarantine laws. It was easy enough,

she knew, to get animals from Australia to Europe, but taking them the other way…

She'd just woken up and here was another instance of Stefanos's arrogance. He'd have planned this before last night, she thought. Before she'd known he was leaving. He'd assumed he could talk her round.

He had talked her round.

But something wasn't making sense. Zoe was up and dressed. She'd gone to sleep—what—at five or six p.m.?

She checked her wristwatch.

Eleven.

She sat bolt upright and yelped. Buster bolted for the far end of the bed, where his new mistress scooped him up and held him close.

'You're scaring him,' she said, reproachful.

'I'm scaring myself. How can it be morning already?'

'It's been morning for ages,' Zoe said. 'I woke up and waited and waited but you kept sleeping. And then I opened the door and there was a really nice lady sitting in the corridor and she said her name was Christina and she'd been waiting for me to wake up. She helped me have a bath—it's a really big bath, Elsa, you should see it—and she helped me with my clothes and then she took me down for breakfast and Stefanos was there. So we had a really yummy breakfast—strawberries, Elsa—and then Stefanos took me to the stables and gave me Buster. And I brought him up to show you but you were *still* sleeping, and Stefanos said we had to let you sleep for as long as you needed to, so we've been really quiet only we've just been watching.'

This was just about the longest speech Zoe had ever made. She sat back on the bed and cuddled Buster the kitten, and Elsa smiled at her in pleasure and wonder. The as-yet-not-met Christina must be good to have Zoe smiling after a bath. To be remembering it with pleasure.

But there was another part of her that was saying uh-oh.

Stefanos was truly seducing them, she thought, watching Zoe's face flush with excitement. He'd already seduced her little charge. Zoe might be hugging her kitten but every time she said Stefanos's name her voice took on the hush of hero worship.

He'd given her strawberries for breakfast. He'd given her a kitten.

Bribery, she thought.

And what was he trying on her?

Seduction of another kind.

But…she kind of liked it.

Matty, Matty, Matty, she thought fiercely but it didn't work. Wherever Matty was, however much she'd loved him, he was no longer protection against Stefanos.

'Do you want to get up now?' Zoe said. 'Stefanos wants to take you out to lunch. He said you both need to talk privately about boring stuff, so he asked if I'd mind staying here with Christina and Buster. And Christina thought she might show me the beach. If that's okay with you,' she added, but her tone said Elsa's agreement was never in doubt.

It couldn't be in doubt. Elsa inspected the request from all angles. There was a lot to consider.

Like going out to lunch with Stefanos. He'd suggested it last night. She didn't remember agreeing.

'He said to tell you it's a picnic. He said to tell you shorts are man…mandatory and swords are optional. I don't know what that means.'

'It means Stefanos is being silly,' she said, a bit too abruptly, and Zoe looked at her in astonishment.

'Don't you like Stefanos?'

'No. Yes! I don't know.'

'Do you want Christina to run you a bath?' Zoe said seriously. 'The bath is lovely. It's really, really deep.'

'I believe I can run my own bath,' Elsa said. 'Though I should take a shower. I hope your cousin Stefanos is taking one too. Preferably cold.'

'Why would he want to do that?' Zoe asked, astonished.

'I have no idea,' she said and summoned a grin. 'I know I'm being stupid. But I think it might be me who needs to take a cold shower.'

She went to shower—but then she changed her mind. This wasn't a place for denying oneself.

Her hip would definitely like a bath.

Back home she survived on tank water. Showers had to be fast of necessity.

Here she had a feeling if she wanted to stay in the bath all day, playing with the amazing selection of bottles of luxury…stuff? no one would say a word of protest. So she did. If not for a day, for almost an hour.

She might have used one too many bottles of smelly stuff, she conceded as she soaked on. She was fighting to keep an airway free through bubbles.

Finally, reluctantly, her conscience got the better of her. She wrapped herself in a fabulously fleecy white towel, used several more towels getting rid of the bubbles and padded back to the bedroom.

She opened her wardrobe and gasped. Yesterday she'd accepted two dresses and a couple of shirts and sandals. Some time during the night her selection had been augmented by…well, by enough clothes to keep a girl happy for a year.

This was really intrusive. She should be angry. But… She tugged out a lovely jonquil blouse and a soft pair of linen shorts. She held them up in front of her and any attempt at anger disappeared.

'If you need to change direction, then you might as well enjoy it,' she told herself, and thought she was about to go on a picnic with Stefanos and she had new clothes and she felt terrific and maybe changing direction wasn't bad at all.

He was leaving.

She wouldn't think about that. She'd cope. She always had coped with what life threw at her. And if life was now throwing bubbles and new clothes at her…and lunches with princes…a girl might just manage to survive.

She came down the staircase looking wide-eyed with apprehension, self-conscious in her neat lemony blouse, white shorts and new sandals—and very, very cute. She'd twisted her curls up into a knot. He liked it, he thought. He liked it a lot.

He'd like it better if he could just untwist it…

'Have you been standing there for hours waiting for me?' she demanded as she saw him.

'Hours,' he agreed, and grinned.

Did she have any idea how cute she was? Her eyes were creased a tiny bit from a lifetime spent in the sun, but that was the only sign of wear. Her nose was spattered with her eighteen gorgeous freckles. If he didn't know for sure she must be close to thirty, he'd have pegged her as little more than a teenager.

And she smelled… She smelled…

'Wow,' he said as she came close, and she grinned.

'Lily of the Valley, Sandalwood and Fig and Anise. There would have been lavender in there too, but I couldn't get the bottle open.'

'Thank God for that,' he said faintly and then counted freckles again. 'Um… Don't you believe in cosmetics?'

'Pardon?'

'Most of the women I know wear make-up,' he said lamely, kicking himself for letting his mouth engage before head.

'Well, good for them,' she said encouragingly. 'Do you, too?'

'Do I what?'

'I've spent so much time in doctors' waiting rooms over the last four years that I've read enough cosmetics advertisements to make me a world expert. There's men's cosmetics as well. I'm sure princes use them. Fake tan's the obvious one. Does your tan rub off on your towel?'

'No,' he said, appalled, and she arched her eyebrows in polite disbelief.

'You'll need sunscreen,' he said, sounding lame, and the look she gave him then was almost scornful.

'Go teach your grandmother to suck eggs. I'm Australian. I put sunscreen on before my knickers.'

And then she heard what she'd said—and blushed.

It was some blush. It started at her toes and worked its way up, a tide of pink. She could feel it, he thought, and her knowledge that it was happening made it worse.

He loved it.

'So...so this is royal beachwear,' she managed, moving on with an obvious struggle.

He glanced down at his casual chinos, his linen shirt and his boat shoes. 'What's wrong with this?'

'Looks great for being a prince and lazing on a sixty-foot yacht on the Mediterranean,' she said. 'It's not great for rock pools, though. And that's where I hoped we'd be going. Somewhere rock pooly?'

She was defending by attack, he thought. But she was still blushing.

Last night he'd kissed her. Right now, all he could think of was that kiss. And how he could repeat it.

He may well get his face slapped, he thought. She'd been way out of control last night, exhausted and vulnerable. Right now...her defences were up and, even if he wanted to—okay, he did want to—she'd be sensible enough for both of them.

'The kitchen staff have set us up with a picnic basket,' he told her. 'There's a great little beach I know a few minutes' drive from here. I believe it even has rock pools.'

'What time will we be back?'

'Does it matter?'

'Yes,' she said, definite. 'I want control here. I should even be deciding where we're going.'

'Isn't it usually the guy...?'

'Who gives orders,' she finished for him. 'I'm sure it is, and if it's a prince then it probably works double. But *Sleeping*

Beauty's for wimps. I fight my own battles—and I set up my own defences. Can I tell Zoe four o'clock?'

'If you like.'

'I do like,' she said. 'You're on probation. After that kiss last night… I don't know why you did it but it scared me. I'm happy to have a picnic but let's make it quite clear this relationship is purely business.'

'Of course,' he said courteously but he was aware of a stab of disappointment.

He didn't know what was happening—but what he did know was that he didn't want to be on a business footing with Elsa.

'So why are we going on a picnic?' she asked as they headed out along the coast road. 'Aren't there urgent princely things you should be doing?'

There were urgent princely things he should be doing, but for now… They were ensconced in a Gullwing Mercedes—a 1954 300 SL. A car with doors that opened like wings from the centre. A car that looked like a weird seagull—a crazy, wonderful car. It had belonged to the King, but it had obviously sat in mothballs for the last fifty years. Finding it had been a highlight of the past two dreary weeks.

And now…it felt great. The sun was shining, they were cruising smoothly around the curves of the scenic coast road, the Mercedes' motor was purring as if it was finally allowed to be doing what it should be doing—and for the moment that was how he felt too. As if he'd got it right.

Beside him… A beautiful woman with freckles.

'So we're going to the beach why?' she prodded again and he shook off his preoccupation with Elsa the woman and Gullwing the car and tried to think of what she'd asked.

'I want to be private.'

'Not so you can kiss me again?'

'No,' he said, startled, and then thought actually that wasn't such a bad idea.

'Just as well,' she said, but her voice was strained. He

glanced across at her and thought she'd come close to admitting that last night's kiss had affected her as much as it had him.

'So you want to talk to me,' she ventured.

'We need to depend on each other,' he said, trying to sound suitably grave and princely. 'Maybe it's time we got to find out a bit more about each other.'

'Without kissing.'

'Without kissing.' Hard to sound grave and princely while saying that.

'So you can figure whether I can take on this island?'

'No.' He grew serious then. 'I'm not asking that of you. It's my responsibility. But I did think—even before last night—that you deserve an explanation of who I am—of what's behind the mess of this island. So that while I'm away you have a clear idea of the background.'

He was manoeuvring the car off the main road now, turning onto a dirt track through what was almost coastal jungle. Once upon a time this had been a magnificent garden but that was a long time ago now. He parked the car under the shade of a vast wisteria draping the canopy of a long-strangled tree. As the car's batwings pushed up, the wisteria's soft flowers sent a shower of petals over their heads.

It was right to come here, Stefanos thought. Matters of state had to wait a little. This felt…right.

Elsa was gazing around her with awe and the beginnings of delight. A tiny stone cottage was also covered with wisteria. It looked ramshackle, neglected and unused.

'This looks almost like home,' she breathed. 'Without the termites.'

'You have termites?'

'My house is wood veneer,' she said darkly. 'Veneer over termites. So what's this place?'

'My home,' he said, and she stared.

'Your home? But you live in Manhattan.'

'Now I do. This is where I was brought up.'

She stared around her, puzzled. 'But a prince wouldn't live here.'

'I wasn't raised as a prince. My father scratched a living fishing. He was killed in a boating accident when I was sixteen. Accidents to the island's original royals are littered throughout our history—never anything that could definitely be attributed to the King, but terrifying, regardless. After Papa died my mother insisted I go abroad. She sold everything to get me into school in the States. Christos left soon after, for the same reasons, only Christos's mother had a little more money so she was able to go with him.'

'So you left the island when you were sixteen? Alone?'

'Yes,' he said flatly. 'I had no choice. Mama was terrified every time I set foot on the island so she insisted I didn't return. She died of a heart attack just before I qualified as a doctor, and it's to my eternal regret I wasn't here for her. I hope…I hope she was proud of my medicine. I've always hoped that what I do was worth her sacrifice.' He shrugged awkwardly. 'Who can tell, but there it is.'

'So…' She was eyeing him cautiously. Sympathetic but wary. 'Why are you telling me this?'

'I want to tell you why I left the island and I want to explain how important my medicine is to me.' He hesitated. 'That's all. Dumb, really. But after last night…it seemed important that you know.'

'You can practice medicine here,' she said, still cautious.

'I can,' he said. 'I will. The old doctor here is overjoyed that I'll be joining him.'

'But…not practising neurosurgery?'

'I'd need a population considerably bigger than this island to justify equipment, technology, ancillary staff. So no.'

'You'll be a good family doctor,' she said softly and he smiled.

'I hope so. If I'm not I'm sure you'll tell me. Now… lunch?'

'Yes, please.'

She climbed out of the car and gazed around her. It was a picture-perfect setting, a tiny house nestled in a tranquil little cove. She thought of Stefanos growing up here, using this place as his own private paradise.

He had it all. His career, his title, his good looks, his life.

So why did she feel sorry for him? It wasn't what he'd intended, she thought, glancing at him as he retrieved a picnic basket from the car. But suddenly... Suddenly she thought she hadn't had it too hard at all.

She'd lost Matty but she'd loved him and he'd loved her. Her own parents had died young but her best friend, Amy, had always been close. And then there'd been Zoe.

How hard must it be to walk alone?

How would he react if she told him she felt sorry for him? she wondered, and then she glanced at him again, at the sheer good looks of the man, the way he smiled at her, the teasing laughter behind his eyes.

All this and sympathy too? This man was too dangerous for words!

He suspected it was a picnic to surpass any picnic she'd ever had. Lobster, crunchy bread rolls, butter curls in a Thermos to keep them cool, a salad of mango and avocado and prawns, lemon slivers, strawberries, tiny meringues, a bottle of sparkling white wine...

'This is enough for a small army,' she gasped as he spread a blanket over a sandy knoll overlooking the sea.

'I doubt the royal kitchen appreciates the concept of enough. Do you think you can make a dent in it?'

'I'll do my best,' she said and proceeded to do just that.

She concentrated on eating, as if it was really important. It probably was, he conceded. She'd missed last night's dinner and this morning's breakfast, but she probably didn't need to concentrate quite as hard as she was.

She seemed nervous, and that made two of them. Last night had left him floundering, and quite simply he didn't know how to go forward. This was a woman unlike any other. A widow. A woman with a past, but a woman who was facing the future with courage, with humour and with love.

Quite simply, she left him awed. And now... He felt as if he were treading on eggshells, and he was already sure he was squashing some.

In the end it was Elsa who broke a silence that was starting to seem strained. 'So tell me about the island,' she ventured. She was lying on the rug looking out to sea. She was on one side of the rug, he was on the other and the picnic gear was in between. It was starting to seem a really intrusive arrangement. But it'd be really unwise to change it, he thought. No matter how much he wanted to.

'I'll show you the island,' he told her. 'When you've finished lunch I'll give you a quick tour. It's far too big to see in a day—but I do want to give you some impression of what we're facing.'

'We?'

'Hey, you offered to help,' he said and then smiled at her look of panic. 'But no, Elsa, relax. I meant *we* as in all the islanders.'

She managed a smile in turn. 'Not *we* as in the royal *we*? Not *we* as in, "We are not amused"?'

'No.'

'So there's still nothing for me to do.'

'There is.' He hesitated, trying to figure a way to say what needed to be said. He couldn't. But still it needed to be said.

'There are three things,' he said at last. 'Some time before I go back to Manhattan—before the end of the month—I'd like to take you to Athens. I want you to buy a dress for the coronation.'

It was such an unexpected request that she looked blank. It was left to him to explain—why he'd woken at three this morning and thought he had to do this. He'd fit it into his schedule somehow.

'I want you to have a gown that'll do justice to your role on the island,' he said simply. 'I want you to stand by Zoe's side at the coronation and look royal yourself. You're her guardian. I'll stand by her side as Prince Regent but you're guardian to the Crown Princess. You should be received with equal honour.'

There was a lengthy silence at that. Then, 'A dress,' Elsa said cautiously. 'You mean…not a nice nannyish dress with a starched collar and Nanny embroidered on the breast.'

'I had in mind more a Princess Di dress. Or a Princess Grace dress. Something to make the islanders gasp.'

'Yeah, right,' she said dryly.

'Yeah, right? That would be two positives? That means you agree?'

'That means there's no way I agree.'

'I wish it,' he said.

'Oooh,' she said. 'Is this insubordination?'

'Elsa…'

'Sorry.' She managed a shaky smile. 'It's an amazing offer.' She shook her head, as if shaking off a dream. 'But it's nuts. For one thing, you have way too much to do to be taking me shopping. How could you possibly justify putting off your surgical lists for something so crazy? And second… The clothes you've already arranged for me are bad enough.'

She faltered then, her colour fading as she realised what she'd said. 'I'm sorry,' she said again. 'I mean…they're lovely and I'm very grateful, but…I don't know how to explain. This is me, Stefanos. I might be changing direction but I'm still me. I don't do Princess Di or Princess Grace. Please. Let me keep being Elsa.'

'You can be Elsa in a couture gown.'

'Yeah, right,' she said again. 'But no. So okay, that's sorted. What next? What else did you want to talk to me about?'

'It would give me pleasure to see…'

'No.' Flat. Definite. 'You're royalty and I'm not. Let's move on.'

Uh-oh. He wasn't having much luck here, and the next one was more important. Maybe he should have voiced it first. Except when he'd thought this all through in the middle of the night, the thought of taking her shopping had distracted him. It was still distracting him.

Maybe now, though, he needed to get serious.

'It's not just shopping,' he said softly. 'I'd like you to see an orthopaedic surgeon in Athens. I want you to get your hip repaired.'

'Now?' she said, astounded.

'Now,' he said. 'You're in pain.'

'I'm not.'

'You are. The pin in your hip hasn't held. You need a complete joint replacement.'

Uh-oh, he thought, watching her face. Maybe he'd gone about this the wrong way.

She stood, staggering a little as she put weight on both feet, but she righted herself fast. Her eyes were flashing fire. 'How do you know,' she said, carefully enunciating each syllable, 'that the pin hasn't held?'

'I rang Brisbane.'

'You rang Brisbane.' The fire in her eyes was suddenly looking downright explosive. 'You mean you rang my treating doctor?'

He was suddenly in really dangerous territory. This woman might change direction at will but she was never going to be compliant or boring or…or less than the Elsa he was starting to have enormous respect for.

Respect? Respect didn't begin to cover what he was feeling.

'You wouldn't tell me what's wrong with your hip,' he said, trying to sound reasonable, but he was wrong-footed and he knew it. He'd wanted to sound caring and concerned and…maybe even magnanimous. Instead, suddenly he was feeling unprofessional and interfering and about the size of a rather small bug.

'So you just asked,' she said, and her anger was starting to make her stutter. 'You thought you'd just ask my doctor what was wrong with me. How did you do that? Did you say, "Hi, Doctor, this is a casual acquaintance of one of your patients. Could you tell me what's wrong with her hip?" Or… "This is Prince Stefanos Leandros Antoniadis from Khryseis and I order you to hand over my servant's medical records." Or…'

She paused for breath. 'Or, "This is Doctor Antoniadis and I have a woman here who can't even get up the stairs without limping so can you send me her records—as one professional to another".'

'It wasn't like that. Elsa, I owe you so much.' He'd risen to face her. Now he tried to take her hands, but she wrenched them away as if he were poison ivy.

'You owe me so much that you can't even grant me privacy?' she demanded.

'I have to know what's wrong with you. Zoe depends on you. We need to get it fixed before I leave.'

'Before you leave... It'll take weeks. Months, even. A week in hospital and at least a month in rehabilitation. When you get back from Manhattan, when things are settled, when Zoe's happy, then I'll think about it. Maybe. Possibly. But it's my business. Mine, Stefanos.'

'Zoe will cope...'

'Zoe will not cope. I will not ask it of her. Now, what's the third thing?'

'I don't think it's wise...'

'I don't think any of this is wise,' she said. 'But ask me anyway.'

'It can wait.'

'I might not be speaking to you tomorrow. Tell me now.'

'It was just...' Hell, he'd messed this. He'd messed this so badly. He wanted to back off but she was waiting, breathing too fast, and he knew that not to finish it would make it even worse than it already was. The third request...

'It's none of my business.'

'So tell me and let me decide.'

He hesitated. But he did need to get to know this woman. Even as her employer, he should know her.

'I'd like you to tell me about Matty.'

'Matty.'

'Your husband.'

'You think I don't know who Matty is?' She seemed almost speechless.

'Of course you do. I'm going about this the wrong way but yesterday… I didn't even know how he died. I should have asked you about him and I'm so sorry I didn't. Matty was your husband and you loved him. He must have been really special.'

Speechless didn't begin to describe how she was feeling. What was it with this man? He'd brought her here for a picnic. He'd fed her lobster and wine—and then he'd talked of buying her ball dresses and phoning her doctor and now he wanted to talk about her dead husband.

Her head was hurting. Her hip was hurting.

She wanted to hit him.

Count to ten, she told herself. Come on, Elsa, you can cope with this.

Personally, Stefanos had overstepped the mark. The knowledge that he'd phoned her doctor and found out information was huge—it threatened to overwhelm her. But that was personal.

Asking her about Matty was personal.

This man was her employer. Nothing else.

So why not tell him about Matty?

It was too confusing. How could she tell him about Matty without betraying Matty? Yet how could the act of telling him about Matty be a betrayal? Unless…unless…

It was far too hard.

'Take me back to the palace, Stefanos,' she said wearily. 'I'm sure you have work to do.'

'But…'

'I have work to do too,' she said. 'If I can't help rule your island, then I'll just have to go back to starfish.'

'There are some great starfish…'

'How many times do I have to tell you—I hate starfish,' she snapped bitterly, irrationally, and shoved the picnic basket aside and lifted the picnic rug and shook it. And if the sea breeze just happened to be blowing in the direction of Stefanos…well, the gods must have meant him to get a face full of sand.

But his phone was ringing and he was retrieving it from his pocket. He didn't seem to notice she was throwing sand at him like a two-year-old having a tantrum.

Frustrated, she folded the rug nicely and gathered the gear together and waited for him to finish.

'Of course I can do it. No, you know I promised. From now on, this is what I do.'

'What?' she said as he snapped his phone shut.

'A two-year-old with croup,' he said. 'In the village near here. Would you mind if we stopped on the way back? Though…it'd mean you miss out on your rock pools.'

Okay, enough of the tantrums. She pulled herself together.

'My rock pools can wait. Of course they can. Croup? Are you working already?'

'Our island doctor has more work than he knows what to do with. I've told him I'll start helping at once. We'll get more medical staff here before I leave, but for now… He's stuck in a clinic on the far side of the island and the child's mother has newborn twins at home and isn't well herself. It's probably just reassurance. If you can wait…'

'Of course I can wait,' she said remorsefully. 'I'm not really a brat.'

'I know you're not a brat. You're…' He hesitated. 'No. Let's just go.'

The drive to the village was done in silence. Stefanos was feeling just about as low as it was possible to feel.

This morning it had seemed a good idea—sensible, even—to take Elsa to the beach. He'd decided to show her he wasn't born a prince—that they had more in common than she thought. He'd offer her a beautiful dress, a shopping trip to Athens. He'd have to push to find time to do it but she needed some sort of gesture to show how much he appreciated her care of Zoe. And…it hadn't escaped his mind that watching Elsa buy a beautiful gown might be a whole lot of fun for him too. Time out for both of them.

The other things had been added because they were also

starting to feel urgent. Every time he noticed her limp now he felt bad. And he needed to find out about Matty.

Okay, the last wasn't essential, but it seemed essential to him—more and more. He didn't fully understand why—it was simply the way Elsa was making him feel.

So he'd set his plan in place and, in doing so, he'd alienated her just about as far as he possibly could.

Good one, he told himself, feeling something akin to pond scum. Only pond scum might have more self-respect.

He knew the place he was going. He drove slowly through the nearby village and hesitated. 'Do you want to come with me? Would you mind staying in the car?'

'I'm happier here,' she said, motioning to the village street. 'I'll poke around and talk to people. That looks a nice peaceful little park. If you take hours, don't worry; I'll be under a tree asleep.'

Once again she'd taken his breath away. He thought of the women he'd taken out before—colleagues, New York singles, women who were smart and savvy and stood up for what they wanted.

So did Elsa, he thought, but only when it was needed. Now...she'd made no fuss, she'd released him from any pressure and he knew instinctively that if it took hours she wouldn't fuss at all.

'Thank you,' he said.

'Stefanos?'

'Yes?'

'I might need a bit of money,' she said diffidently. 'I don't have any local currency and it's been so long since lunch... I might need an ice cream.'

And how good was that, he thought as he drove away. Without any more pressure she'd ensured she had enough money for phone calls and help if he really didn't come back for her.

Only she needn't doubt that. He'd definitely come back for her.

* * *

The old doctor was right—the little boy was suffering mild croup, easily handled at home. What was needed was reassurance and his mother got that in spades, just by Stefanos's presence.

'Our Prince,' the young mother said, over and over. 'Here in my kitchen.'

He smiled and cradled one of her twins and shared a cup of tea with her. As the two-year-old slid into sleep, the young father came home, reacted with awe that Stefanos himself had come, decided his wife obviously needed more support if the Prince himself suggested it and, before he knew it, the children's aunt was unpacking a suitcase in the spare room, fast enough to also join the Prince in yet another cup of tea.

There was nothing to this family medicine, Stefanos thought with wry humour, though his house calls might well need to get a bit faster.

Could he be content with family medicine?

It had its own skills. He was out of date. He'd have to brush up on his general medical knowledge, but he would. It could give him satisfaction. If only...if only the work he'd been doing wasn't so imperative.

Elsa wasn't in the park, but he found her easily. She was standing in front of the butcher's shop, happily licking an ice cream cone, reading the literature in the shop window. With her gorgeous bare legs, her flyaway curls, her ice cream, she stood out like a sunbeam.

'Hi,' she said as he climbed out of his car to join her. Maybe he should get himself a less conspicuous car, he thought ruefully. These wings were crazy. The locals were staring at the car and starting to cluster.

'How goes your patient?' she asked.

'All cured.'

'Really?'

'I'm a fabulous doctor,' he said modestly. 'I prescribed one aunt and lo, the problem's solved.'

'Do they sell aunts in bottles?'

'Sure they do. Can we go?'

'Um…maybe. But have you seen this?' she asked, licking her cone with care.

Woman-cum-eight-year-old. She made him feel…

See, that was the trouble. He didn't know how he felt. *This* was something new, something frightening, something he didn't know what to do with.

'Is this beach far?' she asked.

'What beach?'

'Read the poster,' she said with exaggerated constraint.

He read the poster. It was handwritten, big and to the point.

Turtles hatching. Kemp's Ridley. Lagoon Tempio. Urgent assistance needed—now! Helena.

'Do you know where Lagoon Tempio is?'

'I…yes.'

'Can we go?' she asked. She took a final lick of her cone, decided against more and tossed the remainder in a nearby bin.

'You want to go to this beach?' he said cautiously, aware that the eyes of many people were on him.

'Yes.' To his astonishment, she was suddenly deadly serious. She wiped her hands on her hips and faced him square on. 'Please.'

He stared at the sign. It made no sense. 'Who's Kent Ridley?'

'Kemp's Ridley. Lepidochelys kempii. It's the smallest and most endangered of the world's sea turtles. And they breed together. All the females nest on the one night so hatchings are huge. If it's really Kemp's Ridley… I can't imagine it is, but please, Stefanos, I need to go.'

The sudden passion in her voice stunned him. The vibrant excitement. 'Didn't you tell Zoe you'd be back by four?' he said, astounded at the change in her.

'I told you I told Zoe I'd be back by four,' she said impatiently. 'I was scared you meant a spot of seduction. Stefanos, we need to hurry.'

There was a snort from behind them. The onlookers were

close enough to hear. This was a busy shopping street in the middle of the afternoon and every person here knew who he was. Maybe they didn't know who Elsa was—but they were surely interested.

She'd just made them a whole lot more interested. So many people spoke English these days, he thought.

'Elsa…'

'Okay, I know you didn't want to seduce me,' she conceded. 'You just wanted to ask me a whole lot of questions I failed to answer. But I wasn't to know that. So I'm safe but the turtles aren't. If whoever wrote this poster…Helena?'

'Helena's my mother,' a voice volunteered, and Elsa turned with eagerness.

'Your mother?' She'd slipped easily and fluently into Greek. 'Your mother is saving turtles?'

'They started hatching this morning,' a middle-aged man wearing a butcher's apron told her. 'My mother's excited, too. These turtles used to come here in large numbers—the mass nesting is called an arribadas, my mother says—but forty years ago scientists and tourists were coming to see so the King bulldozed the beach. It broke my mother's heart. But this year… This year they've come back. She wants me to help but I have my shop. I put her sign up in my window but it was all I could do.'

'Does she have helpers?'

'I sent my boy down to help her,' the man told her. 'But there are so many birds… My mother can only save a few.'

'Stefanos,' Elsa said and fixed him with a look he was starting to recognise.

'Yes?'

'As far as I know, there's only one known nesting ground and that's in Mexico. To have a Kemp's Ridley hatching ground right here, where I can help… There'll be a million predators feasting on them. Stefanos, we need a royal decree or something.'

'A royal decree?' he said blankly,

'We have to save those turtles.' She took a deep breath. Steadied. 'Stefanos, if you help me save the turtles, then I'll…I'll…I'll even let you buy me a Princess Grace dress.'

There was a ripple of stunned laughter through the crowd. More and more people were clustered around them now, with more arriving every minute. This was their Prince Regent. And the Princess's nanny.

'So what do we need?' he said simply.

'People. Lots of people.'

She was speaking with passion, and she was waiting for him to act.

People.

'The school,' he said.

'What about the school?'

He turned to the crowd. 'Is the school bus available?'

'It'll be taking the schoolchildren home,' someone told him. 'It should be back here in a few minutes.'

'Who's in charge of it?'

'My son,' someone else called.

'Okay,' Stefanos said. 'I'm commandeering the school bus. Can you tell your son that I'll pay him double the going rate to transport any islander and any child to Lagoon Tempio? There's as much ice cream as they can eat for a week for anyone who comes there.' He grinned at the ice cream vendor. 'I'll reimburse you, and I'll also reimburse you for closing the shop now. That goes for anyone who wants to help.' He glanced at the butcher. 'Phillip, can we set up a barbecue on the beach? If we're going to get people there we need to feed them. Can you contact the baker and Marios at the café? I'll reimburse you for anything anyone eats or drinks tonight. Portia…' he turned to another woman standing by a battered Jeep '…can you take Dr Murdoch there now? I'll pay you for your trouble. By the way, everyone, this is Dr Murdoch—a marine biologist who also happens to be the best thing that's happened to this island for a long time. Elsa, I'll organise things here.

I'll phone the palace and ask that Zoe be brought down to join us.'

He smiled at Elsa. She was all fire and pleading and pure adrenalin, wide-eyed with excitement. He put his finger to his lips and then he placed his finger on hers. 'Let's do this together,' he said and he smiled. 'If only because I really want to see you in that dress. And I'm so sorry I upset you. Okay, everybody, let's go save some turtles.'

CHAPTER TEN

IT TOOK half an hour of phone calls and arrangements before he got to the beach himself—and when he did the sight before him almost blew him away.

Lagoon Tempio was a sheltered cove about fifteen minutes from the village. He'd heard stories about turtles hatching here in the past, but he'd only ever known it as a clear felled, barren stretch of land.

But gradually the land had been recovering. The beach was surrounded by thick vegetation again, a horseshoe cove protected from winds and tides, a perfect place for turtles to come to breed.

Because of the clear felling, it had fallen off most of the islanders' radar. Until now.

He looked down to the beach and there were people. There were so many people his heart sank. Uh-oh. Had he been guilty of overkill?

If Elsa was on a turtle saving mission, maybe bringing this many people here was hardly helpful. Maybe he'd done more harm than good.

He'd encouraged every islander to come, thinking some would take up his invitation. Obviously everyone who'd heard of it had come.

But, even as he thought he'd created chaos, he emerged from the narrow track that led onto the beach—a track that looked as if it had just been created this afternoon by people pushing through—and he saw that he hadn't. Or Elsa and Helena hadn't let it happen.

The adults were in lines, forming corridors from the top of the beach to the water. They were standing like sentinels. Or maybe windmills would be a better description.

For overhead were birds. Hundreds of birds, many of which he didn't recognize—ocean feeders, migratory birds, birds who knew that here was a feast for all.

At the top of the beach were sandy mounds, and from each mound came a stream of hatchings. Tiny turtles, two or three inches across, struggling out of their sandy nests and starting gamely towards the water.

With the mass of seabirds above they'd stand no chance. But now… There were corridors of people from each mound.

He recognised Helena—she was in her eighties, one of the island's stalwarts. She didn't sound eighty. She was booming orders in a voice to put a sea captain to shame—but beaming and beaming.

Alone, she couldn't have saved more than a tiny proportion of these hatchings. But now…

Where was Elsa? Where…?

Finally he saw her, up to her waist in water, in the midst of a group of children. Then, as Helena called out to her, she was out of the water, darting up the beach, pulling people from one corridor to start another.

Hatchlings were coming from beyond the trees at the end of the beach. More mounds? Within moments, Elsa had more adults formed into more corridors. There were islanders arriving all the time and she was using them all.

With her new corridors in place she was off again, back into the shallows, whooping and yelling at the birds above and encouraging the kids to do the same.

Amazingly, Zoe was in there with them, whooping as if she was just one of the kids. The little Crown Princess was yelling and laughing and gloriously happy.

And so was Elsa. She was soaking, dripping with water, laughing at something someone said and then flying up the beach to lift a tiny hatchling which had turned the wrong way, lifting it with a base of sand and then setting it safely near the water's edge so it could meet the waves the way it should.

'Are you here to help?' she called out to him, and he realised he'd been spotted.

'Where do you need me?'

'In deep water,' she called. 'If you don't mind getting wet. I can't get protection deep enough. There are so many turtles. For all the mounds to hatch together...'

'We need boats,' he said and lifted his phone.

'Yes, but meanwhile...'

'Meanwhile I'll do it.' He snapped a command into the phone, tugged off his shirt and shoes and headed for the water.

What followed was an extraordinary evening and night, and at the end of it hundreds—maybe thousands—of baby turtles were flippering their way into the deep, thanks to the islanders' turtle saving skills.

Elsa had moved constantly, working her corridor teams in shifts, making sure no one stayed in the water for more than twenty minutes, a miniature drill sergeant in action. She and Helena had formed a formidable team. Helena was frail, though, and she was almost weeping with joy to have this help.

By dusk Elsa had sent Helena home. 'You've done so much,' she'd told the old lady, and Helena had gripped her hands and wept openly.

'This is thanks to you. To you and your prince. I thank you.'

Embarrassed, Elsa had headed back into the water and stayed there.

As the afternoon turned to evening, as Phillip's barbecue faded to cinders, as the mass of turtle hatchling eased and finally it could be left to a dozen people taking turns, he finally dragged her off the beach. He made her dry herself, almost force-fed her a steak and an apple and watched over her while she ate.

'I should be back helping,' she muttered, impatient.

'You can be. But not now. Not until you've had a break.'

Someone had brought a vast mound of pillows and blankets. Zoe and a couple of other island children were lying cocooned in blankets, watching the flames, giggling sleepily to each other. He recognised one of the children as Phillip's daughter—a child about the same age as Zoe. They were lying side by side. It seemed Zoe was making a friend. She looked…happy.

So was Elsa. She was flushed and triumphant and glowing.

The scene was weirdly domestic. Family? In his mind was suddenly a piercing stab of what he'd once had. A longing…

'Did you see them?' Elsa said softly, speaking almost to herself. 'We saved thousands. They face so many dangers in the water but now… Thanks to Helena, they have a chance.'

'Thanks to you.'

'Helena was on her own,' she whispered. 'She's been watching the mounds. If one mound had hatched she would have had a chance to save some. She hadn't realized, or she'd forgotten, that Kemp's Ridley turtles lay their eggs in synchronisation so they all hatch together. There'll be another hatching in twenty-five days—that's set as well. I've worked it out—that's before your coronation so you'll still be here. Kemp's Ridleys lay in synchronisation twenty-five days apart. Isn't that amazing? Aren't we lucky?'

She looked up at him then, and she smiled. 'But it's you,' she said on a note of awe. 'You're a prince. The islanders moved today because you asked them to. If they'd thought about it—if Helena had had the time to individually plead—then maybe she'd have got half a dozen people to help her, but you said come and they came. They came because of you and I can't thank you enough.'

'There's no need for you to thank me.' He was watching her and he was feeling…weird. She was slight and feisty and sand-coated and bedraggled.

He'd hurt her today. He hadn't meant to but he was starting to realise how he'd got it so wrong. And why. She was tugging his heart strings in a way he didn't recognise. Or maybe…in a way he did but until now he'd been afraid to face.

'Do you know how rare these turtles are?' she said softly. 'I can't believe it. They're so endangered. To have a breeding site on this island... I so wish Matt was here.'

That set him back a bit. Pushed what he was thinking to the side.

It didn't completely obliterate it, though.

Even if she didn't tell him about Matty... He could compete with someone who'd died four years ago, he thought, and then realised where his thoughts were taking him and thought who cared; they were going there anyway.

'This is wonderful,' she said softly into the firelight. They had the fire almost to themselves now. The children were nestled in their beds on the far side of the barbecue but the rest of the islanders had either gone home to rest or were back on the beach on their shift. 'I can stay here,' she said. 'I can do so much work here.'

'What about your starfish?'

She looked startled. 'What about my starfish?'

'Have you really lost your enthusiasm?'

She looked at him as if he were a sandwich short of a picnic. 'Enthusiastic about starfish?'

'According to Zoe, it's what you love.'

'I love Zoe.'

'You don't love starfish?'

'As opposed to Kemp's Ridley...' Her voice was awed. 'Kemp's Ridley turtles on an island where my Zoe needs to be. This is awesome.'

'But your research...'

'I can work around that, too,' she said. 'I've already handed over my initial starfish research—there were any number of students just aching to take it on. But if I can do this and keep Zoe happy... There's so much. Helena says there are plans for development of this beach. Something about moving the town's refuse station close by. She's worried.'

'We can protect this beach.' He hesitated. 'And...I hope we can get tourism going. The island's desperate for income.'

'It's hardly touched,' she whispered, looking out through the trees where the lights of a score of torches showed the turtles still had safe passage. 'It could be the best eco resort. Matt and I had such plans…'

There it was again. Matt.

Maybe this was going to be harder than he'd thought.

Maybe what was going to be harder? He knew. More and more, he knew. He watched her face and he thought he wanted this woman so much…

It was too soon. Way too soon. Stupid, even?

'Okay, we have that settled,' she said, not noticing his silence. 'I'll stay here and love Zoe and save turtles. You'll have to figure your own direction, but I have mine.' She rose and wiped her hands on her shorts—a gesture he was starting to recognise. 'Let's move on. If you'll excuse me, I have work to do.'

'I'd be honoured to help,' he said. 'And…I will be here long-term. I will be part of this island. Elsa…' He reached out and took her hands.

She stood, looking down at them in the firelight. The linking of fingers.

'Not a good idea,' she whispered.

'We could work this together.'

'Sorry?'

'It's just a thought.'

'I'm quite happy for you to help with the turtles any time you want,' she said and he knew she was deliberately misunderstanding him. 'But for now… Your patients and the islanders need you, and the turtles need me. Zoe needs me. That's enough for one girl, wouldn't you say, Dr Antoniadis?'

'Steve.'

'Prince Stefanos,' she retorted, still watching their linked hands. 'My employer.'

'I'm not your employer.'

'Why, what else would you be?' she asked and she carefully untangled their fingers. Separated their hands. Took a step back and looked at him with eyes that were carefully watchful. 'I need to go back to the beach. Will you stay here and watch over Zoe?'

'I'll go back to the water. Your hip must be hurting.'

'My turtles are important,' she said. 'They're my job. Let me have that at least,' she retorted and, before he could respond—before he even knew how to respond—she turned and headed back down to the beach.

Leaving him to try and figure where to take things from here.

He stared down at the fire—and then focused. Heading for the flames were three tiny turtles.

How had they made their way back here? They'd built this fire purposely far back from the beach, out of sight of the mounds, so the light couldn't distract the hatchlings from their course. Maybe these three had been distracted by a torch, had deviated from their course and ended up here. He scooped them up before they could get close enough to the fire to harm themselves.

'Elsa?' he called into the night and in seconds she was back. Looking straight to Zoe.

But Zoe slept on. Elsa's face slackened in relief, and he thought how much had she worried? How many infections, dramas had she endured during these four years of getting Zoe back to health?

'It's just turtles,' he said swiftly and she looked down at his hand. He had one hand cupped over the other but tiny flippers were peeking through. They felt weird. A handful of flippering.

'They were just…here,' he said, in case she thought he'd collected them from the beach, done something less than noble, he didn't know what, but he was starting to suspect she thought he wasn't exactly hero material.

Hell, he wished he could be.

'What in the world are they doing here?' she asked, opening his hands and taking them into her smaller ones with all the tenderness in the world. 'Hey, guys, the ocean's this-a-way.'

'I guess, if they walked far enough, the ocean is that-a-way,' he said.

'Yeah, but changing direction's easier,' she whispered. 'I ought to know. Come on, guys, I'll take you where you need to go.'

'What do you mean, changing direction's easier?' he asked.

She looked up at him in the firelight and shook her head. 'If you need to explain it, you can't do it,' she said. 'You just…follow your heart. Thank you, Stefanos, for saving my turtles. And thank you for giving me another direction. I'll make the most of it.'

'Your hip…'

'Has nothing to do with direction,' she said. 'Some things still hurt, no matter what direction you're travelling.'

CHAPTER ELEVEN

FOR the next three weeks she immersed herself in this new life and felt herself...unfurl. That was what it felt like, she thought. As if she was coming to life again.

For the last four years she'd been constantly worried, constantly battling for their survival. Here, Zoe's welfare was more than taken care of. It was Stefanos who inspected the little girl's grafts, who worried about her medically, who even told her to back off a little, she was fussing. Others cooked for her, cleaned... Elsa was an honoured guest, free to do as she wished.

And she was free. Zoe had made a friend her own age, Pip, daughter of Phillip the butcher, granddaughter of Helena, defender of the turtles. She was friends with every one of the castle staff now, she was happy and confident and more than content that Elsa do her own thing.

So Elsa was making her own friends. The turtle breeding grounds was a project which had her waking up every morning aching to get up and go.

The only problem was...in the moments when she'd sit opposite Stefanos at meals and watch his face as the palace secretary outlined what needed to be done that day, she felt...bleak.

He was doing the right thing, the honourable thing. But, for Zoe and for her, this new life promised excitement and freedom. For Stefanos... There was still a conflict that seemed to be tearing him apart.

She didn't know what was happening with his practice in Manhattan. The plan was to leave straight after the coronation and do what needed to be done and return. She tried to talk to him about it, but it was as if after their appalling picnic he'd decided he'd overstepped the boundaries; his life was separate, only overlapping with her need to be with Zoe.

Oh, his bleakness wasn't overt. Outwardly he was cheerful and confident and purposeful. It was only that she seemed to know this man; she seemed to sense how he was feeling.

His trouble was the one cloud on her horizon. Actually, no, sometimes it felt more than that, like a fog she could see rolling in to envelop him, but she had no idea what to do about it. The fact that sometimes she had an urgent desire to take him and hold him and love him… Well, that was just plain dumb.

And…she suspected it might not even help.

Meanwhile, the coronation was almost on them, and she'd made her promise. It was time to buy a dress.

Zoe's coronation dress was exquisite, stitched by hand by a team of dressmakers who smiled all the time they worked, who said what a pleasure it was to be able to do this, what a joy. So, 'Can't I get my gown made here as well?' she asked Stefanos, knowing how stressed he was and how little he could spare the time to be away.

But, 'It's my one bright day,' he said. 'I think I've worked hard enough to earn one free day.'

He surely had. What he'd achieved in these last weeks was little short of miraculous.

The island council had been reformed. Three councillors had been invited to stay on; five had been 'retired'. Stefanos had done it with tact but with an underlying ruthlessness that left her awed.

The governance of the island was now under the control of the council, with ultimate responsibility resting with Stefanos. The royal coffers were being used with a speed that made her blink. Advertisements were already appearing on the mainland, for teachers, for engineers, builders, nurses…

Unemployment on the island had been running at over fifty per cent. No longer. There were schools and hospitals to build, roads to repair, water mains to install, electricity to supply to the inland area…

'Giorgos and his predecessors have held on to our taxes for hundreds of years,' Stefanos told her when she questioned how the island could possibly afford what he was starting. 'Alexandros on Sappheiros has split the royal coffers into three so there's more than enough to get things moving.'

He worked with a ruthless efficiency that left her awed. But still there seemed to be this aching need…

She heard him, late at night. Her balcony overlooked the sea and so did his. She'd walk outside to watch the sea and she'd hear him talking, discussing operations, questioning results, talking to colleagues about cases they needed his help with.

He was needed elsewhere. He was working frantically so he could leave, fitting in as much medicine as he could as well. He'd found a locum to work here while he was away, to leave him free.

And he'd come back. He'd promised that he'd come back. But he didn't want to. She heard it in his voice—that coming back would tear him in two.

And she couldn't help.

But first…her dress.

'I've organised a seaplane to pick us up and take us to Athens for the day,' he'd told her at dinner the day before.

Three weeks ago Zoe would have reacted to this proposal in fear. Now she simply looked up and said, 'Am I coming too?'

She'd been tucking into her dinner as if she had hollow legs. The difference in her health since she had been here was astonishing.

'I've asked Pip's mama if you can stay with Pip for the day,' Stefanos said. 'Is that okay?'

'Ooh, yes,' Zoe said, pleased.

'And Pip's mama says it's okay if Pip comes back here and

sleeps for the night. Christina will look after both of you and you'll have Buster to keep you company. I thought I might take Elsa shopping in Athens for something beautiful to wear to our coronation, and I thought I might take her to dinner afterwards.'

From the start he'd been able to wind his cousin round his little finger and this was no exception.

'Elsa would like that,' Zoe said seriously. 'She says she doesn't like dresses, but she does really. And boys are supposed to take girls out to dinner.'

'Hey,' Elsa said, startled. Half laughing, half horrified. 'I'm here. It's not like you're talking behind my back.' But she was ignored.

'It'll be a date,' Zoe said in satisfaction. 'You have to kiss her on the way home.'

'Who says?' Elsa demanded.

'Pip's big sister went out on a date last week. Pip says when the boy brought her home he kissed her goodnight.'

'Pip's sister is eighteen,' Elsa retorted. 'I'm too old for that nonsense.'

'You're not,' Zoe said seriously. 'You're still quite pretty.'

'Gee, thanks.' She hesitated. 'Stefanos, it really isn't necessary.'

'You promised,' Stefanos pointed out. 'A bargain's a bargain. I've saved your turtles. Twice.'

He had, too. The second hatching, twenty-five days after the first, had been orchestrated so that, as far as they knew, every single hatchling had made it to the water. It was a fraught journey the turtles had before them, the sea was full of dangers, but Stefanos had done everything humanly possible to see they had every chance.

And the price? A snip. An agreement to buy a dress.

'Athens or nothing,' he said. 'It has to be special.'

'All right,' she said grudgingly.

'You're very gracious,' Stefanos said and he was laughing at her. Laughing!

At least the bleakness had lifted for the moment.

That conversation had taken place last night. And now...

Stefanos was waiting in the hall. A car was waiting to take them down to the harbour, to the seaplane.

In minutes she'd be climbing aboard an aeroplane with a prince...

'Are you coming or do I have to come up and carry you down?' he called from below in the entrance hall.

She went.

There was something about this day that made her feel...dizzy. Sitting in the seaplane across from Stefanos, she stared straight ahead.

'Are you okay?' he asked gently, fifteen minutes into the flight, and she nodded but couldn't even find the courage to answer.

This was one day out. A shopping expedition for a dress, followed by a meal.

Why did it feel so overwhelmingly scary?

Stefanos smiled at her and retired to a medical journal. Medicine, she thought. He missed it so much. Or...he missed his own niche of medicine.

He was already busy helping the elderly doctor on the island with his workload. It wasn't the medicine he was trained for, but that was the medicine he was reading up on.

Finally they were there. Athens! It was all she could do not to sit with her nose squashed against the car window.

Athens. The world.

'Not a seasoned traveller?' Stefanos teased, and she flushed.

'Sure I am. I just like looking.' And then, as they swung off the road into a huge car park, she frowned. 'Where are we?'

'It's a hospital,' he said. 'I've arranged an appointment for your hip.'

'Stefanos...' She was almost rigid with shock. 'You've interfered enough.'

'No,' he said. 'Not enough. I know I handled this badly. I

know I should have gained your permission before I accessed your records, but what's done is done. I'm sorry but if I'd told you about this appointment I was afraid you'd refuse to come.'

'You'd be right.'

'Then I'm justified.' He hesitated, but his look was stern. 'Elsa, this is only a doctor's appointment. I'm not chaining you to a bed and operating regardless.' He gave a rueful smile. 'Actually, that might be beyond even my level of intrusion. But I am one of only two doctors on Khryseis and before I go back to New York I need to know you're not doing permanent damage. This man's an orthopaedic surgeon. The best in Athens. You need to see him.'

'You still should have asked me.'

'I'm asking you now. This is my honour, Elsa, and it's also sense,' he said, stern again. 'I know I upset you—obtaining your medical history without permission—but it doesn't stop the need. I need you to do this—for you. It would be childish for you to refuse—no?'

'No.'

'Elsa... You *will* do this.'

She had no choice. He was right—she was being childish but it didn't make it any easier to swallow her temper. She followed him into the hospital, fuming.

He was recognised. Doors opened for him. The receptionist of this best-in-Athens-orthopaedic-surgeon practically genuflected.

'You can go right in, Your Highness. The doctor's expecting you.'

But, to her surprise, Stefanos didn't go in. He simply smiled at her, gave her a gentle push towards the door and settled his long frame into a waiting room chair as if he had all the time in the world.

She stared down at him, stunned.

'What?' he said, looking up. And then, 'He won't bite, Elsa. I thought, as he might want to examine you, I should stay out here. But if you're scared...'

The door was opening behind her. She wheeled round and an elderly doctor was smiling a greeting.

'Dr Murdoch. Come on in.' And then he smiled across at Stefanos. 'Steve. Welcome home. When are you coming home for good, my boy?'

'By Christmas.'

'But not to work in neurosurgery?' the older man said, looking suddenly concerned. 'I've heard you'll let that go. I had this young man working with me for a while as he was training and I was in the States,' he told Elsa. 'It was an honour and a pleasure to work with one so talented.' He turned back to Stefanos. 'But now…to abandon your neuro-surgery… There must be some way you can fit that into your new life.'

'There's not,' Stefanos said. 'The island's far too small.'

'Could you work in Athens? There's a need here.'

'No,' Stefanos said abruptly. 'Please…leave it. It's Elsa we're concerned about here. Not me.'

'But what a waste,' he said softly. And then he turned back to Elsa. 'Well, then. What has to be has to be. Meanwhile, come with me, young lady, and let's see what needs to be done about that hip.'

He was, as Stefanos had promised, very good.

He examined her with care and with skill. He already had the X-rays from Brisbane—a fact that made Elsa gasp again with indignation but that shouldn't reflect on this kindly doctor. She let him take his time, carefully assess and then tell her what she wanted to hear.

'You're doing no real harm to the hip itself, but it does need to be repaired and it will give you pain until that happens.'

'So I can wait,' she said thankfully. 'Can you tell that to Stefanos?'

'You want me to call him in?'

'Yes, please,' she said, tugging on her shoes. 'Tell him and let me get on with my life.'

So Stefanos came in. He listened while the doctor outlined exactly what he thought.

'But you know this,' the doctor told Stefanos. 'You've seen the scans.'

'I'm too close to treat Elsa myself.'

'You are,' the doctor said gently. 'And you'd need first rate surgical facilities on that island of yours to be able to do it. You know, that's what you really need. A state-of-the-art suite of operating theatres. Cutting-edge techniques. All the things I hear you're doing in New York.'

'And an island like Khryseis would support that how?'

'I have no idea,' the doctor said sadly, and he turned to Elsa and smiled. 'This man tries to save the world and I wish I could help him. But of course he's right. We can only do what we can do. So let's do that, young lady. We need to get your surgery scheduled. When?'

'But you just said…'

'I said the operation's not urgent. That means it doesn't have to be done as soon as possible. The only way to keep you pain-free is to give you so much opiate as to risk addiction, and I suspect you made the decision some time ago to live with the pain. But, because it's hurting, you're not weight-bearing evenly. That will cause long-term back problems. There's tenderness already in the lower spine and I'm concerned there'll be too much pressure on the muscles around the lower vertebrae. So when can we schedule surgery?'

'We can't,' Elsa gasped.

'I can be back here in seven weeks,' Stefanos said, ignoring her. 'Can we schedule it just after Christmas?'

They left the hospital grounds without speaking. Elsa should have been furious. She tried to dredge up fury all the way to the shops. But instead she simply felt bleak. The cab stopped, Stefanos paid, she got out and looked around her—and she decided there and then to cheer up.

She was here shopping. For a gorgeous dress. This was obviously where the wealthy women of Athens shopped.

Indignation—and bleakness on Stefanos's behalf—would have to wait until later.

'What are we waiting for?' she said. 'Do you have the royal credit card?'

'I believe I do.'

'Then let's not let the little pet get cold,' she said and dived happily into the first shop.

It was as if her visit to the doctor had unleashed something in her that had needed to be unleashed for a long time.

Her exultation—dizzy bordering on hysteria—lasted until she was standing in front of a mass of mirrors wearing a gown that fitted her like a second skin, crimson silk, shimmering and lustrous, flecked with strands of glittering silver. The gown had shoestring straps, the bodice clinging and curving around her lovely body, then falling in generous folds to sweep the floor. She gazed into the mirror in incredulity. She met Stefanos's gaze in the mirror and stared at him as if he were part of the same fairy tale.

Then she seemed to come to earth with a crash. She dragged her gaze from his—and lifted the price tag.

And yelped.

'We'll take it,' Stefanos said, and grinned as her mouth dropped open. He'd obviously put aside his bleakness as well. 'One gown down, half a dozen to go—dear,' he said.

'D...dear?' she spluttered.

'Sorry...' he said, and smiled.

The salesgirl was looking on with incredulous delight. 'You want more?'

'Maybe the others don't need to be quite so formal,' Stefanos decreed. 'But we do want at least three more. And what about some sexy lingerie to go with them?'

'Sexy lingerie!'

'It's in the royal nanny dress code,' he said, straight-faced. 'Don't tell me you haven't read it?'

'But I don't need...'

'You do need.'

'What about your Third World kids?' she demanded. 'Don't you need all your money for them?'

'They're not watching,' he said. 'Quick, buy.'

'Stefanos…'

'Tell you what,' he said with magnanimity. 'For every dollar you spend on your wardrobe I'll donate ten more to my Third World medical network. I can't say fairer than that, now can I? So if you refuse to spend, you're doing an orphan out of medical treatment.'

'Stef…'

'You want to start calling me Steve?' he asked, and suddenly his tone was gentle.

'No,' she said and then, more strongly, 'no. You're Stefanos. Prince Stefanos. And I'm the nanny. But I'm a nanny who won't say no to a dress or two.' Then she blushed. 'Or…or even lingerie. But, Stefanos…'

'Yes?'

'You know when you stayed outside while I saw the doctor?'

'Yes.'

'Step outside, Your Highness,' she said, smiling sweetly. 'In the interest of Third World aid, I need to discuss knickers.'

He'd booked them into a hotel. At first she was incredulous. The taxi dropped them outside the most lavish hotel she could imagine. She stared out at the ancient Grecian columns—how had they incorporated them into a modern hotel?—and then she gazed back at Stefanos.

For a moment she said nothing. And then… 'Ten times the cost to a Third World orphan?'

'You have my word,' he said solemnly. 'My orders are for you to have fun tonight. That's all I ask.'

'I'll wear my second best frock,' she said. And then, more cautiously still, 'I didn't think we were staying the night. I don't have a toothbrush.'

'I believe these things are obtainable for a small fee,' he said. 'Multiplied by ten, of course. And you did buy enough

lingerie to keep you respectable—or maybe not respectable—
for a month.'

She blushed. 'How did you know I bought…?' He'd been
out of the shop. 'How…?'

'You gave me the receipt,' he told her. 'So I could multiply
by ten.'

'Right,' she said and blushed some more. Then, 'Okay. So
I'll buy a toothbrush.' Then she had another thought and her
blush moved from pink to crimson. But somehow she made
herself sound stern. 'But it's definitely separate rooms.'

'Separate suites,' he corrected her.

'Oh, of course,' she said and suddenly she giggled. 'This
is ridiculous.'

'I have a feeling there hasn't been enough ridiculous in your
life.'

'I don't need it.'

'You know, I'm very sure you do,' he said gently. 'And
maybe the same goes for me. Maybe we both need a good dose
of crazy.'

They ate by candlelight in the hotel restaurant, with a view
over all of Athens. A view to die for. Food to die for.

A man to die for.

The set-up was so corny she half expected an orchestra to
materialise at any minute and strike up with *Love Me Tender*
or something equally soppy. And, just as she thought it, a
pianist slipped behind a grand piano and started playing. Not
Love Me Tender—but close. She was wearing her second best
dress, which was a fantasy of Audrey Hepburn proportions.
Pale lemon silk with tiny white polka dots. Tiny waist, huge
skirt. Cleavage.

She'd twisted her hair into a casual knot, trying for
Audrey's look. She thought she looked a bit scruffy for the
Audrey look, but Stefanos's long, lingering gaze when he'd
come to her room to accompany her downstairs said she didn't
look scruffy at all.

She was still nervous. Stupidly nervous.

'Should we be talking politics?' she asked as the waiter
brought them plate after plate of food she'd never tasted before
but would taste forever in her dreams.

'No politics.'

'About Zoe, then.'

'No children.'

'About your medicine? My turtles?'

'Nothing,' he said softly. 'Just you.'

'Well, there's a boring night,' she said, feeling breathless.
'There's nothing to talk about there.'

'We could dance,' he suggested as the pianist started a soft
waltz in the background.

'Right. And my hip?'

'Let me dance for you,' he said. He stood up and held her
hands and tugged her to her feet.

'I can't.'

'You can. Take your shoes off and put your feet on mine.'

'That's ridiculous.'

'Not ridiculous at all. Trust me, Elsa. Dance with me.'

Then he took her into his arms—and waltzed.

He moved with the effortless grace of a panther, a dancer who
knew every move and who knew how to take her with him.

She hadn't danced since she'd injured her hip. She'd hardly
danced before then, but it didn't matter.

Her feet were on his. He was holding her weight so her
hip didn't hurt, so she could move with him, as one with
him, in this slow and lovely dance, as if she weighed
nothing.

How had she got herself here? She'd agreed to buy one
dress and now…she was being seduced.

Seduced?

No. This was payola for what she'd agreed to do. He was
giving her a very nice time.

And if it was seduction… She didn't care, she thought
suddenly. What did it matter if her employer seduced her?
Employers did these things. Princes did these things.

Um…no. Elsa Murdoch didn't do these things.

'Did you dance with your husband?' he murmured into her ear…and the fairy tale stopped, right then, right there.

'Pardon?' She froze in his arms. Her feet slipped off his and she could have cried. She was on solid earth again and the lovely dance had ended.

'I didn't mean…'

'To remind me of Matty? I'm very sure you did.'

But he was looking confused. As if he'd been in a kind of dream as well.

'I did dance with Matty,' she said, jutting her chin. 'We danced very well.'

'You loved Matty?'

'With all my heart.'

'And you grieve for him still?'

'I…yes.' What was a girl to say to that, after all? But something went out as she said it—a light, an intensity in Stefanos's gaze.

And its going meant grief. How could she say she'd loved her husband but she was ready to move on?

How could she think it?

'You'll dance again when your hip's healed,' he was saying softly.

'I won't,' she muttered, coming back to earth with a crash. 'I shouldn't.'

'Elsa…'

'I don't want to think about Matty,' she whispered. 'Not here. Not with you.'

They were alone on the dance floor. There were maybe ten or so tables occupied, but the lights were low, the other two couples who'd danced with them to begin with had left, and there was now just the two of them. The pianist had shifted from waltz music to something soft and dreamlike and wonderful.

There was nothing between them. Only a whisper of breath. Only a whisper of fear.

'Elsa…' he murmured, and her name was a question. His

hands slipped from the lovely waltz hold so they were in the small of her back.

'Elsa,' he said for the third time, and he bent his head...and he kissed her.

It was a long, lingering kiss, deep and wonderful, hot and warm and strong, demanding, caressing, questioning.

It was a kiss like she'd never been kissed before.

She was standing in the middle of a dance floor, her arms around his neck and she was being kissed as she'd always dreamed she could be kissed.

She was being kissed as she'd wanted to be kissed all her life.

Matty...

Stefanos himself had pulled her husband into the equation. He was with her still—maybe he always would be. His kisses had been just as wonderful, but different—so different, another dream, another life. He wasn't stopping her kissing right back.

This was the most wonderful dream. Her hip didn't hurt, her worries about Zoe were ended, she wasn't responsible for anything, for anything, for anything...

He was lifting her so he could deepen the kiss, cradling her, loving her and she thought her heart might well burst, as she realised she was so in love with him.

In love with him.

She, Elsa, was in love with a prince. Wasn't Cinderella only in story books?

And, almost as soon as the thought was with her, the spell was broken. People were...clapping?

She twisted, confused, within the circle of Stefanos's arms and found the tables of diners were all watching them, smiling, applauding.

'It's Prince Stefanos from Khryseis,' someone called out in laughing good humour. 'With the Princess's nanny.'

Oh, right. She pulled back as if she'd been burned and Stefanos let her go to arm's reach. But he was still smiling. Smiling and smiling.

'Not the nanny,' he murmured. 'Elsa.'

'In your dreams,' she muttered and it was so close to what was real that she almost gasped. Not in his dreams. In *her* dreams.

'Stefanos…'

'I'm falling in love with you,' he said, simply and strongly and she gasped again.

'You can't. I'm just…'

'You're just Elsa. You're the most beautiful woman I've ever met.'

'You're kidding me, right?' she demanded. 'I have freckles.'

'Eighteen.'

'Eighteen?'

'Eighteen freckles. I love every one of them. Elsa, I've been trying to figure where we can take this.'

'Where we…'

'If we were to marry,' he said and her world stilled again.

'M…marry?'

'I didn't come prepared,' he said ruefully. 'I should be going down on one knee right now, with a diamond the size of a house in my pocket. But I've only just thought of it. Alexandros said I needed a wife, and he's right.'

'You've had too much champagne.'

'No,' he said and then, more strongly, 'no! I know what I want, Elsa, and I want you.'

'Because Alexandros said.'

'I don't think I did that very well,' he said ruefully. 'Believe it or not, it's far less about Alexandros than about eighteen freckles.'

'Eighteen freckles are hardly a basis for marriage.'

'I believe you're wrong,' he said gravely. 'But we could work on other attractions. Do you possibly think you could love me? I know you loved Matty. I know you still love Matty. I'll always honour that, but…is it possible that I could…grow on you?'

'Like a wart?' she said cautiously.

'Something like that,' he agreed. He smiled and, chuckling, pulled her close.

But... But. This might be the magic she'd longed for but there were buts surfacing in all directions.

'Stefanos, no.' She tugged away again, trouble surfacing in all directions. They were being watched, she knew, but the piano was still playing softly in the background and maybe they were more private here than if they went back to their table.

'Will you be my wife?' he asked, solidly and strongly, and there it was, a proposal to take her breath away.

The *but* was still there. Forcing her hand.

'No,' she said.

'No?'

'I'm not changing direction again.' She stood, mute and troubled. 'Not...not while you don't know where you're going.'

'I do know where I'm going.'

'You don't.' She was frantically trying to think this through. To be sensible when she wanted to be swept away in fantasy. Only fantasy was for fairy tales and this was real. 'Stefanos, the problem is...you've committed yourself to staying on the island and you're making the best of it. But that's not what I want. You making the best of it.'

'It's not such a bad deal,' he said, puzzled. 'If it includes you.'

'I'm not the consolation prize.'

'I would never suggest...'

'No, you wouldn't,' she whispered. 'Of course not. You're too noble and too wonderful and too...' She hesitated. 'Too just plain fabulous. The problem is, Stefanos, that even though I'm falling in love with you—and I am—I can't see you tied even more to the island. Tell me...you're thinking...or you have been thinking...that maybe you can take some slabs of time away. Maybe you can do some teaching. Not when you're needed on the island, of course, but if we can get more doctors, if the politics are settled... You're thinking that, aren't you?'

'Yes, but…'

'But I don't think that'll make you happy,' she said. 'I think that's going to tear you further apart. For you'll lose your skills. You'll see others go where you want to go.' She hesitated. 'Stefanos, when Matty died and I couldn't do what we were doing with coral any more… I know it sounds simplistic and silly in the face of what you're doing but it was important to me and I couldn't just do a little bit. It would have eaten at me. I had to move on.'

'I think,' he said steadily, 'that in marrying you I would be moving on.'

'I won't be the cause,' she said. 'In no way.' She bit her lip. 'Stefanos, do what you have to do and then decide you want to marry me. If you were to do that…'

'I am already.'

'You're not.' She shook her head. 'I can't make you see. I don't even know whether I understand it myself, but in the bottom of my heart it does make sense—that I say no. That I say wait. That I say loving is…for when it's right.' She hesitated. 'Matty and I…'

'Matty?'

'You asked me about Matty,' she said. 'Maybe I do need to tell you. Just as we finished university Matty inherited his father's company. His mother sobbed and said he had to come home and run it. So he did—his entire extended family seemed to depend on him and it seemed the only right thing to do. He loved me so I went with him, but it almost destroyed us. For two years I worked on my research while Matty self-destructed. And in the end he handed the entire company over to his cousins. It left us broke. His family thought he was mad. But, you know what, Stefanos, the one thing I do know… When he was killed I thought of those wasted two years.'

'You're saying…'

'I'm saying I don't want the heartache of those two years again, Stefanos. Oh, I want you. I don't deny I want you— my love for Matty hasn't stopped me feeling more for you than I ever thought I could again. But I will follow my own drum and I won't watch you self-destruct while you follow someone else's.'

'So what do you propose I do?' he said bleakly.

'Work it out,' she said steadily. 'For yourself and for me. Please, Stefanos.'

He didn't understand. He was seeing her distress, but not seeing it either, she thought. Maybe he was only seeing what he wanted to see. The Cinderella bit. The fantasy.

Whereas what she wanted was more. Love at first sight? No. Love for ever.

All at once she felt tired. Weary of the pain in her hip, weary of worry, weary of the pain inside her heart.

It'd be so good to do just what she wanted, she thought. To have the world magically transformed so she could sink into her prince's kisses and let herself have a happy ever after.

Stefanos.

He was fighting to change the world, she thought. He was fighting himself.

She didn't have the courage to stand by his side as he did it.

It was too much. Too soon. Too scary. It was yet another direction, but this one was so big, so terrifying that if she got it wrong it could destroy them all. And if she didn't get it right…if she wasn't sure, if she jumped with her heart before her head said it could follow…where would that leave them all?

Oh, but she wanted to.

She mustn't.

'I need to go to bed,' she whispered. 'You've paid me the most extraordinary compliment…'

'A compliment! It's so much more…'

'It is, isn't it?' she whispered bleakly, and she stood on tiptoe and kissed him lightly on the lips. A feather touch. A kiss he didn't understand. 'I know you don't follow what I'm saying—I hardly understand what I'm saying myself. I only know that…I don't know if I can face your demons with you,

Stefanos. Maybe I need more courage than I have. Goodnight and thank you. And I love you.'

And, before he could respond, she'd turned and fled from the dance floor. She didn't stop until she reached her suite, until she was inside with the door locked behind her.

CHAPTER TWELVE

ON A sun-kissed afternoon in early November the Crowns of Khryseis were bestowed on Zoe and on Stefanos.

Crown Princess Zoe of Khryseis was seated on a throne too large for her. Her dress was pure fantasy. She looked adorable. She looked very, very scared.

Only the fact that her cousin was standing right beside her gave her the courage to stay. Stefanos, Prince Regent of Khryseis, the Isle of Gold, had vowed to defend his little cousin, care for her and cherish her and take care of her interests until she reached twenty-five years of age.

Stefanos looked magnificent. Zoe looked exquisite.

Elsa was looking not too bad herself, she conceded, thinking what a waste, why spend all this money on her fabulous gown if her nose was about to turn red? But she was fighting tears, and Crown Princess Lily of Sappheiros glanced sideways at her and smiled and passed over a handkerchief.

'This is dumb,' Elsa whispered, embarrassed. 'I shouldn't be here in the front row with you. I'm not even royalty.'

'Hey, I've only been royalty for a couple of months now,' Lily said. 'And, from what I've heard, you're even closer to Zoe than Stefanos.'

Elsa sniffed. The Archbishop was watching Stefanos sign before his little cousin now. It looked so official. It looked like another world.

She could have been up there. Beaming and waving and being royal too. As Stefanos's wife.

Her reasons for refusing him were sounding weaker and weaker. It was just as well he hadn't proposed again, she thought. Any pressure and she might well cave right in.

'He's gorgeous,' Lily whispered thoughtfully, watching Elsa's face.

'He is.' She looked dubiously at the handkerchief. 'I need to blow my nose.'

'Go right ahead,' Lily said grandly. 'I came supplied with hankies in bulk. They're monogrammed with the royal crest.'

Elsa nearly dropped it. Lily giggled and suddenly Elsa was smiling again, albeit through tears. What was royalty but individuals doing the best they could? The vows that Zoe and Stefanos had just made… They weren't taking them away from her. Or no further than they already were. And she was right not to join them. Her doubts still stood.

The signing was done. The orchestra was starting its triumphant chorus, a blaze of sound proclaiming that Khryseis finally had its own royal family.

Stefanos helped Zoe to her feet. Zoe stood, looking out nervously at the vast audience in front of her.

Stefanos held her hand, stooped and whispered to her.

Zoe stared up at him, then out at the people in front of her. And then, at a signal from Stefanos, the music suddenly died.

Zoe took a deep breath. She turned back to Stefanos, as if for approval of something prearranged, and she looked straight at Elsa.

'I need my Elsa,' she said in a high, clear voice. 'Elsa, can you come up and walk beside me?'

'Quick, blow,' Lily muttered urgently. 'And your nose isn't even red. You're beautiful.'

He walked out of the cathedral behind them. Zoe and Elsa. His little cousin and her beautiful guardian.

Elsa's eyes were looking distinctly watery. He wasn't surprised. His eyes were feeling distinctly watery too.

Elsa should be walking by his side. It felt wrong.

He'd rushed it. He'd pushed her too hard, too fast, ripping her out of her comfort zone, asking the world of her and then asking her to extend that world.

Zoe was happy again. She'd been coached with care and kindness, and she knew exactly what was expected of her today. Elsa had raised her beautifully, he thought. When she'd spoken her responses it had been with the gravity of one twice her age. So much of that was down to Elsa's care, her constant assurances that Zoe was beautiful, that the scars and the pain were only skin deep and what was underneath was beauty and joy.

If he'd got it right he could have been walking down the aisle with Elsa, with Zoe between them.

He'd messed it up—badly.

But he had time, he thought. He could try again.

Only Elsa was right. His doubts about what he was doing were still there.

Khryseis needed him.

His work in Manhattan was still calling.

Elsa had the courage to change direction and move steadily forward. He kept glancing back.

Elsa knew him better than he knew himself. And, knowing him, she had the sense not to want to be his wife.

'Isn't Stefanos beautiful?' Zoe was so close to sleep she could barely form words, but she'd stayed until the last speech had been made, she'd sat attentive and courteous, and Elsa was so proud of her she was close to bursting. But now she'd retired to Elsa's knee for a hug, the hug had turned into a cradling cuddle and it was clear the little girl just wanted to drift off to sleep.

They were watching Stefanos say farewell to the dignitaries. Stefanos as they'd first seen him, only grander.

'I don't have to be scared of being a princess when he's here,' Zoe whispered. 'I wish he wasn't going away.'

'Me, too,' Elsa whispered. For what the heck; there was no point in lying, not even to herself.

'Do you think he'll come and live with you and me for ever and ever?'

'He's said he will. Maybe not with us but near us.'

'That's good,' Zoe whispered, her whisper fading so that Elsa could hardly hear. 'But I'll miss him and miss him. And so will Buster.'

'And so will I,' Elsa told her and watched her close her eyes and drift off into sleep. 'I think I might miss him so much I might have to think about changing direction all over again.'

Only of course there was no time for direction changing. No opportunity. No chance.

A call came through that night. Stefanos needed to be in New York within twenty-four hours.

There were so many things to do, documents to sign, authority to delegate… He moved as fast as he could. Elsa woke at dawn to a light tap on her door and it was Stefanos, come to say goodbye.

She stood at her bedroom door in her lovely new lingerie, feeling shocked, bereft and stupidly frightened.

'You will come back?' she murmured. She must have sounded needy for Stefanos took her hands in his and tugged her into his arms before she could resist.

'Of course I'll be back. I'll be here by Christmas.'

He was as she loved him most, in his casual jeans, an old leather jacket slung over his shoulder, unshaven, a man in a hurry. 'Hell, Elsa, I wish I didn't have to go. But these kids… I can't knock them back.'

'I so wish you could work from here.'

'And we both know that I can't.'

'Of course.' The population of Khryseis could never support the medical facilities this man needed.

'You'll keep Zoe safe. And our turtles. And Buster.'

'I promise.'

'Christmas in Australia's hot, isn't it?' he said. 'You think we can do an Australian Christmas dinner?'

'Amy's Christmas Cake,' she said before she thought about it.

'Amy's cake?'

This was crazy. Standing in her bare feet, talking to a man she loved with all her heart about her best friend's cake.

'It's a berry ice cream cake,' she said. 'Amy was so proud of it—it was a tradition started by the women in her family who couldn't bear a hot Christmas pudding. She'd start a month before Christmas, finding berries, then building layer upon layer of berry ice cream, each layer a different flavour. By Christmas we might have ten layers. Then we'd turn it out and decorate it with more berries. She'd make a berry coulis to pour over. It was so big sometimes it'd last until well into January.'

'So you make it every year?'

'Not…' She hesitated. 'Not since Amy died. Berries are expensive.'

'I see,' he said gravely and took her hands in his. 'Then here's my royal decree. You use the royal card again to buy as many berries as you need—import them, grow them—whatever you have to do to get them, you get them, and make us Amy's Christmas Cake. And we'll eat it well into January.' He was smiling into her eyes and his smile might as well be a kiss. And…she felt like crying.

'Is there anything you want me to bring from New York?' he said, maybe seeing her need to be practical, to get over the emotion. As if she could.

'Come home via Australia and bring me my cats,' she said, trying desperately to joke. 'I miss them.'

'It's a bit of a detour.'

'You're the Prince Regent.'

'So I am,' he said and smiled his crooked, heart-flipping smile, then stood looking down at her for a long, long moment as his smile faded. A door slammed below stairs, someone called to him and he swore.

'I have to go. Will you say goodbye to Zoe for me? I can't wake her yet.'

'Of course I will. Travel safe.' She smiled. 'I was teasing about the cats.'

'I know you were.' He gave an almost imperceptible nod, as though her cats and his safety were inconsequential. As if there was something more important he'd decided to say. 'Elsa...'

'Just go.'

'I will,' he said, but instead he tugged her close and she had neither strength nor will to resist. He pulled her tight into his arms, against his chest, and he kissed her, hard and long and aching with need.

And then he put her away from him.

'G...go,' she managed.

'I love you,' he said, loudly and strongly into the morning.

But still he turned. And he went.

She wanted to sob. Or maybe something louder. She'd actually quite like to stomp a bit. Toss the odd pillow.

Yell.

But Zoe and Buster were fast asleep. She should be, too. What else was she to do?

She needn't worry about breakfast. It would be on the table in a couple of hours, a choice of eight or so dishes, eat what you like and certainly don't worry about the cost.

She was Zoe's friend and guardian, only Zoe already had a friend. After Christmas Zoe would try the little school that stood just by the castle gates. What was a woman to do then?

Research her turtles and don't deviate. Become a world authority. Stay facing in the one direction...

Hope Stefanos could find a direction too, one that could fulfil his dreams, and hope with everything in her heart that his direction matched hers.

She loved him.

There wasn't a lot she could do about it. Flying out of the door wailing, *Wait for me, wait for me,* would hardly be appropriate or sensible or even possible.

So.… Go back to sleep until it's time for the royal day to begin.

Start making Amy's Christmas Cake.

Wait for her prince to come home.

It was a direct flight from Athens to New York. The details of his surgical list had been faxed through to him so he had a mass of reading to do on the way. He leafed through the first case and then the second—and then found himself staring sightlessly ahead. Superimposed on the printed pages was the vision of Elsa's tousled curls, her bare feet, as she'd opened the door to say goodbye.

More than anything else he'd wanted to sweep her into his arms, take her back to her bed and stay with her for ever and ever and ever.

She'd knocked back his proposal of marriage. He was trying to understand her reasons.

He'd spoken too early. One night in Athens hadn't been enough. Her hip had been hurting. He needed to have her healed and then take her away properly—a weekend in Paris, maybe. Or a month in Paris.

Or New York? There was his dream. Manhattan and Elsa. Or…more, he thought. Manhattan and Elsa and Zoe and Buster. His family—something he'd never thought he wanted, but now he had such a hunger for that he couldn't see past it.

But… He had to stay in Khryseis.

And that was the problem, he thought. Elsa knew better than he did that marriage to her would make things better for him. But she'd knocked back his proposal. He had to make things better himself.

'Excuse me, but are you Prince Stefanos of Khryseis?'

The man in the next seat had been glancing at him covertly since take-off. Small, a bit unkempt, wearing half-rimmed glasses and the air of a scholar, he'd been reading notes that looked even more dense than those Stefanos had been studying.

'I am,' Stefanos said warily, because admitting to being royalty was usually asking for trouble.

'So you're the one who seduced our Dr Elsa from her studies.'

'Pardon?' What the hell…? This man looked angry.

'She's brilliant,' the man said, ignoring Stefanos's incredulity. 'She has one of the most brilliant scientific minds in Australia. In the world. She and that husband of hers…the research they did on the preservation of the Great Barrier Reef was groundbreaking. If she'd kept it up it could have made her a professor in any of the most prestigious universities in the world. And then she just hands it over. Hands it over!'

'I don't know what you mean,' Stefanos said.

'Her work,' the man said impatiently, and then suddenly seemed to remember his manners. 'David Hemming,' he said. 'Professor of Marine Studies at… Well, never mind, it doesn't matter. All I know is that I've never seen such a generous act. She had all the research done. All the hard work. She was just starting to see the academic rewards and suddenly a letter arrives out of the blue saying she can no longer go on with her studies but she doesn't want her research wasted so here it is, take it and publish as you see fit, just take it forward. Well, I tell you there's at least eight international experts now who are international experts only because of Dr Langham's generosity.'

'Dr Langham?'

'We could never find her,' he said morosely. 'Only then we started hearing about starfish research—really interesting stuff—and dammit, there she was, only she was calling herself Elsa Murdoch. But, just as we were finding out what she was doing, dammit if she didn't do exactly the same again. Package it all up and pass it on. No honours for her. Just good, solid research that'll mean species will survive that were otherwise facing extinction. And now…'

He'd been building up indignation, incense personified, and Stefanos got poked in the chest with a pencil. 'And now she's off again. But at least it's turtles this time. Kemp's Ridley, by what I hear, and you couldn't get a better woman working on them. You know what? She sees the big picture. Already she's contacting international institutions, trying to broaden our understanding. If she's found this breeding site there must be more. She'll use that to make them safe.'

'How…?'

'Pure energy,' he said, stabbing Stefanos again. 'Only don't you let her give her work away this time. If she settles—if she's allowed to settle—then I'm guaranteeing those blessed turtles will be safe for a thousand years, such is the commitment she generates. So you might have seduced her to your island but you make sure she stays. Or I and half the marine academics in the world will want to know why not.'

And, with a final poke in the chest, he retired back to his notes.

Leaving Stefanos winded.

Stunned.

The vision of Elsa as he'd last seen her was still with him— beautiful, almost ethereal, a freckled imp with her glorious sun-blonded curls. With her face creasing from laughter to gravity, from teasing to earnestness, from joy to…love?

To loss.

If he'd met her when she was twenty, when life was simple, when she was free to fall in love, then maybe he'd have stood a chance. He knew that. For he'd looked into her eyes and what he saw there was a reflection of what he believed himself. That she was falling in love with him as deeply as he was falling in love with her.

Only life had got complicated. He'd thought it was complicated for him. How much more complicated was it for her?

She'd buried a husband. She'd said goodbye to two careers. She'd taken on a child so injured that she'd needed almost a hundred per cent commitment, and that at a time when Elsa was injured herself.

And along came Prince Stefanos, grudgingly changing direction this once. Hating the idea that he'd be handing over his work, his teaching, his skills, watching others take his work forward while he ceased to be able to contribute.

She knew his commitment was grudging. She had so much generosity of spirit herself that she must know it.

He'd enjoy family medicine, he thought, and doing everything else he could to help Khryseis, as a doctor and as the island's Prince Regent. He must. He'd immerse himself into it all, convince Elsa that he was content.

Only she knew him. He couldn't lie to her. And it wasn't entirely the work he wanted to do.

Khryseis wasn't big enough for the medical work he wanted to do.

But…

For some reason, the academic's words stuck. Hit a chord. *You know what? She sees the big picture.*

Khryseis was one of three islands. Put together…

He needed to concentrate on these cases. He'd be operating hours after landing. He needed to read his notes.

But there were things happening in his head apart from his most pressing concerns. Major things.

The image came to him of the night he'd held the three tiny turtle hatchlings in his hand.

I guess, if they walked far enough, the ocean is that-a-way, he'd said.

Yeah, but changing direction's easier, she'd whispered. *I ought to know.*

Could he somehow change direction but get to the same place by another route?

There wasn't time to think this through now. Those kids were lined up waiting for him. But he had six weeks to think.

How much did he want Elsa?

And Zoe. And Khryseis. And turtles and cats and Amy's Christmas Cake which, for some weird reason, was becoming a really big thing to look forward to.

How much did he want them all?

He lifted his third set of case notes and tried to read.

But all he saw was Elsa.

CHAPTER THIRTEEN

THEY coped without him.

It was a strange thing, caring for a child who'd been dependent for years but who was finally finding her wings. Zoe couldn't wait to get out of bed in the morning, to meet her new friend, to play with Buster, to be allowed to start school. Medical constraints, always suffered stoically, were now a nuisance to be ignored. She bounced around the palace with growing confidence and pleasure, and by Christmas there wasn't a member of the palace staff who wouldn't have given their right arm for her.

Zoe was gloriously in love with this new life.

So was Elsa. Sort of.

She and Helena were working through the issues with the turtles with cautious exhilaration. There was so much to be done. The turtles' habitat had been destroyed once, and only part of it had regrown. Turtles were crossing roads to dig their nests. There were threats everywhere, and this for a world endangered species. Making them safe was imperative. Extrapolating the research was breathtakingly exciting. She could make a difference.

There were so many things she could do.

But she wanted to be with Stefanos. Every morning she woke rethinking his proposal. Was she crazy? She'd turned down a man she could love with all her heart.

She knew it was more than that, but that was the problem. Her head knew things her heart didn't necessarily agree with.

'Will Stefanos be home for Christmas?' Zoe asked for about the thousandth time since he'd left and, for the thousandth time, she replied.

'He said he would be. He's phoning us as often as he can, sweetheart, and he doesn't seem to be changing his mind. And then he's going to stay with you while I have my hip fixed.'

'I don't want you to go away.'

She didn't want to go away either, but it was organised. The day after New Year she'd fly to Athens and spend a month in hospital.

She should be grateful. She was grateful. Zoe was happy and blooming. There were no money problems. She had work that truly interested her, and her hip was about to be treated.

So why was a part of her so miserable?

Happy Christmas, she told herself fiercely on Christmas Eve, as she helped Zoe hang her stocking in front of the vast fireplace in the great hall. Last year she'd used a sock in front of the fire-stove. This year the housekeeper had hand-stitched Zoe a gold and crimson stocking, with the most beautiful appliquéd Father Christmas and elves and reindeer.

It looked beautiful on the great mantel. But, despite the massive Christmas tree the staff had set up—or maybe because of it—it looked really alone.

'You should have a stocking too,' Zoe said as she'd said every Christmas since they'd been together.

'Stockings are for kids.'

'You never get presents.'

'Stefanos should be home. That'll be a present for both of us.'

'He should be here now,' Zoe said severely. It was almost bedtime on Christmas Eve. She'd counted on her big cousin coming today. 'He said he'd come.'

'Maybe he'll come in the night like Santa Claus,' Elsa said. 'Maybe we won't see him come if we stay up.'

'You think we should go to bed?'

'Why not?' She was weary of waiting, herself. She was

iding an emotional roller coaster and didn't know how to get
off. If Stefanos didn't come... He'd promised Zoe.

He'd promised her.

'Okay,' Zoe said, infinitely trusting. She tucked her hand
into Elsa's and tugged her towards the stairs. 'Let's go to bed
and make it come quicker.'

He had so much to do he felt like Santa Claus, zooming across
the world at midnight. Actually he was only flying from
Athens to Khryseis on the seaplane, but he did feel a bit like
Santa. He had so many gifts in his pack. He sat next to the
pilot, gazed out at the blue-black sky and the stars hanging low
and lovely in the heavens, and he felt that a little bit of magic
was around.

He needed magic. In his pocket was a ring almost worthy
of the woman he loved—the ancient ring of Khryseis, plaited
gold with three magnificent diamonds embedded in its depths.

She wouldn't take it unless she accepted the rest of his
sleigh load, he thought ruefully. A woman of principle was the
woman he'd chosen to give his heart.

Would she take it? He'd done so much. If there was
anything else he could do... Anything at all...

He had a mad compulsion to tell the pilot to turn the plane
around. So much was at stake. The woman he'd chosen as his
life's partner had knocked him back because of her principles.
If he didn't get it right this time...

What else could he do?

The lights of Khryseis came into view and the plane started
its descent. He could see the palace from here, lit up like a fairy
palace. That'd be the staff celebrating Christmas, he thought.
The whole staff—the whole island—was overjoyed to have
their royal family in residence.

Or their royal princess and her nanny, he corrected himself.
For a family required more.

Would she accept him now? She must. For years he'd
scorned the idea of a family. Now it seemed he couldn't live
without it.

He'd met one feisty, beautiful nanny and his world had changed.

'Coming in to land now, sir,' the pilot said, looking ahead at the palace lights. 'Seems someone's keeping the home fires burning.'

'I hope so,' he murmured.

'I think every person on the island hopes so,' the pilot said enigmatically. 'Welcome home, Your Highness.'

'Santa's been and Stefanos is home.'

Elsa woke to find Zoe bouncing up and down on her bed, the long-suffering Buster being bounced with her. 'Come and see, come and see, come and see. Santa's been, Santa's been, Santa's been.'

Despite the tumult of emotions she'd gone to bed with and woken with—*Stefanos is home*—she had to smile. Zoe had been just as excited last year when all she'd been able to give her were a couple of handmade toys she'd bought at a local market. This year should be fun.

Stefanos is home.

'It's humungous,' Zoe was saying. 'You should see. How can Santa have brought it down the chimney?'

Humungous? Nothing she'd stuffed in Zoe's stocking could be described as humungous. And…

Stefanos is home.

'Stefanos…' she said cautiously.

'He got home really late. Christina told me he snuck in after all the staff went to bed—almost morning. Elsa, you have to get up and see what Santa's brought me.'

So Stefanos would be asleep. That gave her breathing space. She'd have time to enjoy Zoe's stocking with her before she needed to face him.

It wasn't that she didn't want to see him, she thought, feeling really confused. Not exactly. There was a big part of her that ached for him.

There was another part of her that was just plain custard.

But he was asleep. Hooray. She threw back the covers, pulled on a robe and padded downstairs.

She'd never get used to the opulence of this place. The staircase was wide enough to fit ten people abreast.

'The king who built this place must have been as fat as a whale,' she told Zoe. 'Or he had ten kids to take by the hand every Christmas morning.' Zoe giggled and they were both still chuckling as Zoe hauled open the double doors to the great hall.

She stopped dead.

How long since she'd believed in Santa Claus?

When they'd gone to bed the Christmas tree was a decorator item, set up by the staff as a tasteful ode to Christmas. Now…whoever had come during the night had turned the tree into an over the top muddle.

The exquisite decorations and silver lights were still under there somewhere, but they were now almost hidden. Hung over the top of them were rows and rows of coloured popcorn, threaded together and hung in vast ribbons of garish colour. There were paper lanterns—every colour of the rainbow. Pictures of cats had been placed in tiny silver frames and hung as ornaments. There was a collection of motley socks hanging everywhere, all bulging.

'The socks have got apples in them,' Zoe said, awed, tugging her towards the tree. 'That one's a football sock and that one has a hole in the toe. And look at my present.'

She was seeing it. Stunned.

It was a trampoline, an eminently bouncy mat, built with a net canopy around it so a child could bounce without fear of falling.

For a child who needed to be encouraged to stretch scar tissue…for a child who loved bouncing…it was the best thing.

'And you have a stocking too,' Zoe said, deeply satisfied. 'Look.'

She looked. On the mantelpiece hung three stockings. Zoe's was bulging with nonsense gifts, a tin whistle, a boomerang—a boomerang?—a clockwork mouse…

More pictures of cats.

And there was a stocking labelled *Elsa*. A small parcel bulged in the toe, a document rolled and tied with a huge red bow was sticking out the end, and there were more pictures of cats.

The stocking labelled *Stefanos* was empty.

'We should have something for Stefanos,' Zoe said anxiously. 'Santa didn't come to him.'

'We have a couple of gifts in our room,' Elsa said uncertainly. 'We could sneak up and put them in his stocking before he wakes.'

'It's too late for sneaking,' said a low gravelly voice and she yelped.

The voice had come from behind the vast Christmas tree. Zoe darted behind in a flash.

'Stefanos,' she shouted. 'He's here. Elsa, he's here, sleeping behind the tree.'

'I always sleep behind the tree,' a sleepy voice murmured, full of laughter. 'For years and years. But I've never yet caught Santa Claus. Has he come?'

'He's come, he's come.' Zoe was squealing with excitement. 'And he's brought crazy socks. Elsa, he's here. Stefanos is here. Come and see.'

There wasn't a choice. She should have at least brushed her hair, she thought desperately, as she tried to organise her smile to be cool and welcoming. She walked cautiously around the tree, and there he was. He'd hauled a mattress downstairs, and a mound of bedding. He was lying back, smiling up at them, his blankets pulled only to his waist. Bare-chested.

Breathtakingly gorgeous.

Buster was on his stomach already, kneading his blankets with her soft paws and purring so hard you'd swear she'd recognised him. Zoe was snuggling down beside him, a little girl with everything she wanted in life.

'You've messed with our Christmas decorations,' she muttered before she could stop herself, and his grin widened.

'I threaded popcorn all the way from New York to Athens,

and I made half my fellow passengers help me. The rest were on lantern duty. And then it still looked a bit empty so Santa had to resort to socks. And a happy Christmas to you too, Mrs Murdoch. Dr Langham. My love.'

There was a bit too much in that statement for Elsa to think about. She opened her mouth to reply and gave up and closed it again.

'No Happy Christmas?' he said, smiling at her evident confusion.

'Happy Christmas,' she managed, sounding winded. 'Why…why aren't you in your own bed?'

'I might have missed present opening. Have you opened your stocking yet?' He rolled out of bed. He'd gone to bed wearing boxer shorts. Only boxer shorts. What more could a girl want for Christmas? she thought as she watched him stretch and yawn; as she thought all sorts of things that surely a nicely brought up girl—a mature widow!—had no business thinking.

Had she opened her stocking? 'N…no,' she managed, annoyed that her voice squeaked. 'It's bad form to open gifts until the family's together.'

'Is the family together now?' he asked gently and he looked at Zoe cradling Buster and then he looked to her with such an expression that her heart did a double backflip. Landed on its back. Refused to start operating again in any mode she considered normal.

'I…I guess,' she muttered.

'No guessing,' he said, suddenly stern. 'You need to be sure. Zoe, I'm assuming you've guessed this very fine trampoline came squeezing down the chimney in the wee small hours especially for you. Would you like to try it out for size?'

'Ooh, yes,' Zoe said and flew with Buster to the trampoline, only to be hauled back by her big cousin.

'Buster,' Stefanos said firmly, removing the long-suffering kitten from her arms, 'stays on the ground.'

Only he didn't. Stefanos handed Buster to Elsa and then, when her hands were safely occupied and she couldn't fend him off, he kissed her. Just the once, but the look in his eyes said there were more where that came from. Just the once, but it was enough to light her world.

'It appears I'm needing to send out a royal decree for mistletoe,' he growled, his lovely crooked smile warming parts of her she hadn't known were cold. 'Honestly. Can't you people be depended on to organise anything?'

She managed a chuckle but it was a pretty wavery chuckle. She was too…thrown.

'Happy Christmas,' he said again, and then obviously decided mistletoe was not absolutely essential and he kissed her again, deeply this time, long and hard and so wonderfully that finally Zoe ceased bouncing, put her hands on her hips and issued a royal decree of her own.

'Yuck,' she said. 'And you're squashing Buster. Stop kissing and open presents.'

'Yes, ma'am,' Stefanos said and swept Elsa—and the slightly squished Buster—into his arms and deposited them both on the settee by the tree. Then he lifted the rolled document out of the top of her stocking and handed it to her, with such gravitas it was as if he was handing over royal title to his land and his kingdom for ever.

She looked up at him, wondering, but he was looking grave and expectant, waiting for her to discover for herself what it was. Slowly she unfastened the ribbon holding the roll of documents together. Buster pounced on the ribbon; she set both ribbon and Buster on the floor and then looked up at Stefanos again, half afraid to go further.

'Well, go on, then,' he said, in the same tone of impatience Zoe had just used. 'Read it.'

She read.

… Transfer of title of Diamond Mine Number Two on the Isle of Argyros, the income from which to be used in perpetuity for the health of all the citizens of the Diamond Isles…

She stared up at him, confused. He smiled back at her, and he didn't look confused in the least.

'I'm changing my direction,' he said softly. 'So I'm hoping…if I head in the same direction as you, can we walk together?'

'I…I don't know what you mean.'

He sat down beside her, took the documents back and set them aside. His face was suddenly grave. 'Elsa, on the plane on the way to New York I met a man who knew you. He told me about your research, and you know what else he said about you? He said… *She sees the big picture.* And he spoke in awe. He meant you don't just look at the turtles on the beach that need saving. You broaden your work; you look at their survival internationally. And I finally figured it out. It was like I'd needed a swipe to the side of the head to wake me up, and I finally got it. That's what I've been guilty of. Seeing only what's before my eyes. Not thinking big. Seeing only my work in Manhattan and how much it means.'

'But your work is important,' she said, confused, struggling to understand.

'It is,' he agreed, still grave, laughter put aside as he tried to make her see. 'Elsa, without conceit, I can say my work changes lives. So when I knew I had to work here I was gutted. I knew I had no choice—the islanders are my people. And then there was a new imperative. You're my people. You're my family, Elsa. You and Zoe. I want you so much—and it was such a shock to realise I ached for a family. I ached for you. I was so committed to what I was feeling for you, and to the needs of the islanders as well, that I'd stopped thinking big. It took one stray remark about how wonderful you were to make me rethink.'

'I don't think I'm following your logic,' she managed cautiously, trying to focus on his words rather than the joy and love she was seeing in his eyes. The joy and love that was building inside her. She didn't know yet what he was talking about but the smile behind his eyes said it was good.

'We're too small.' He had her hands now, holding her tight. 'But now I'm thinking big. Elsa, this document is a plan.'

'Something about a diamond mine?' she ventured. Good one, Elsa. Intelligence wasn't on the agenda this morning—nor was speed reading. All she was seeing was Stefanos.

'Absolutely it's about a diamond mine, my love,' he said and tugged her into his arms and kissed her again. Long and lingering and lovely. But then he set her back from him. There were still things that needed to be said.

There were things she didn't understand, and he had to make her see.

'There are six diamond mines on Argyros,' he said softly while she listened in wonder. 'Argyros is therefore the wealthiest of the Diamond Isles but it has no hospital. Nikos has been talking to me about setting up decent medical facilities there. It's the same on Sappheiros—Alexandros is already making plans for a hospital. And then, on the plane, I made myself see the big picture. Separately we're small islands. We each need good medical facilities but we don't each have the population to set up a major base. But together...'

'Together?'

'It's too big,' he said ruefully. 'To land this on you on Christmas morning. But I can't wait any longer. Elsa, I love you, I want you more than life itself, but I've already asked you to marry me. What I need now is for you to know I've changed. Everything's changed. Except my love for you. So...can I tell you what we've decided? The rulers of the other two islands and me?'

How was a girl to react to that? Her heart was starting to sing. Bubbles of happiness were floating to the surface and filling the room with joy. 'I'm...I'm listening,' she whispered, and suddenly so was Zoe, sitting cross-legged on her trampoline, watching with big, serious eyes. She really was much older than her eight years, Elsa thought, and then she thought that, whatever was coming—and already joy was starting to overwhelm her—it was appropriate that Zoe was here. To bear witness, she thought, and then she thought that was a dumb thing to think but she thought it anyway.

'Earth to Elsa,' Stefanos said, laughing softly and tightening his grip on her hands and she thought, okay, thoughts could come at some other time. Now was the time for listening.

'It's a medical scheme,' he told her, and in his eyes was jubilation, excitement, a man about to embark on a *Boy's Own* adventure. 'A medical centre second to none will be built, here on Khryseis, with satellite hospitals on the other two islands. Fast and easy transfer facilities. Every specialist we need. Together we'll care for the people of the Diamond Isles as they deserve to be cared for. It's what I dreamed of as a kid, as did Alexandros on Sappheiros, and Nikos on Argyros. Three Crowns, Elsa. Three Crowns finally come together to provide care for all.'

'One…one big medical centre?' She was struggling to take it in.

'State-of-the-art. And, with the islands being as lovely as they are, and the salaries we're prepared to pay, we don't expect any trouble staffing them as they should be staffed. We don't see islanders needing to go to Athens for treatment any more. We see mainlanders coming to us.' His hands moved to her shoulders, holding her, desperate for her to share his joy.

'Alex and Nikos flew to New York to work this through with me. For such a project, for something so wonderful for all of us, the diamonds on Argyros will be needed, but none of us can see a better use for them. We envisage offering our medical facilities worldwide. And more. There'll be resorts on each island that are half hotel, half hospital. Come here and be pampered and made well, and support our economy while you do.'

He was so exultant now his excitement was practically blazing. 'We've done the preliminary figures and the guys in suits agree with us,' he told her. 'It *will* work. And here's the tail, Elsa. Here's my huge joy. With the money raised we believe we can still bring people here from Third World countries. I'll be able to operate as I've been doing and I'll be able to teach. So...so what do you think?'

He paused then. He was still holding her by the shoulders, his eyes not leaving hers. But now...his excitement faded a little, giving way to anxiety.

He was asking what she thought? *He was anxious about what she'd think?*

'You'd be here,' she whispered. 'You'd be doing the work you love.'

'I'd be doing all the work I love,' he said, excitement giving way to gravity. 'I'll be ruling this island in Zoe's stead, caring for it as it must be cared for. I'll be doing the medicine I love—I'll be making a difference. And I'll be sharing my life with you.'

'With me.'

'And with Zoe,' he said, his eyes lighting with laughter again. This much joy couldn't be contained for more than a moment. 'And our cats.'

'Cats,' she said cautiously, for she was starting to see a theme here. There were pictures of cats all over the Christmas tree. 'Cats, plural?'

'I made a few calls to Australia,' he said. 'I figured...well, I hoped you might be staying here long term, and the guy feeding your cats now has twenty-three on his list.'

'Twenty-three...' she gasped.

'It seems he's Waratah Cove's answer to the Pied Piper of Hamelin. He's taken them on as his mission in life.'

'Don't tell me you're bringing them here,' she managed.

Zoe said, 'Ooh!'

'That's not an ooh,' Elsa said, torn between laughter and horror. 'It's an Are You Out Of Your Mind?'

'I hoped you might say that,' Stefanos said, smiling into her eyes with such a look that she might, just might, be forced to forgive him twenty-three cats—or anything at all. 'So what I've done is give the guy a job in perpetuity, caring for them all. With one exception.'

'One...'

'A skinny little black one,' he said apologetically. 'I met him that first day when you guys were on the beach and I had to find you. It seems he's been pining for you—he's hardly eaten since you left and, to tell you the truth, I sort of fell for him. So he's on his way here as we speak. My love.'

My love. There was enough in those two words to be perfectly adequate, thank you very much—she hardly wanted more.

Only Zoe was made of sterner stuff. She darted across to the mantelpiece and was flying back, tipping the contents of Elsa's stocking at her feet.

'You have another present and I have six. Maybe I ought to open some of mine first.'

'If you don't mind, Zoe,' Stefanos said and lifted the tiny crimson box from where it had fallen. 'So far Elsa's just had paper. You have a trampoline and this is important.'

'Elsa has a cat,' Zoe said.

'Yes, but he's not here yet. So, as yet, she's giftless.'

'Okay,' Zoe said obligingly, grabbing the long-suffering Buster and squatting beside Elsa. 'But it's really small. Open it fast, Elsa.'

'Open it slow, Elsa,' Stefanos said, and watched as Elsa forgot to breathe and tried to make fumbling fingers operate the catch of the tiny box.

'Let me,' Stefanos said at last, and flicked the clasp. And there, resting on a bed of black velvet, was the most beautiful ring she'd ever seen. It was gnarled and twisted gold, burnished with age and history, with three magnificent diamonds set in its depths—diamonds to take a girl's breath away.

'It's the ancient ring of this island, worn by the ruling Princess of Khryseis for generations,' Stefanos said softly. 'On her marriage. If…if you'd like to be married, that is. If you'd like to be my princess.' He took a deep breath. 'If you'd like to be married to me.'

'It's beeyootiful,' Zoe breathed, but Elsa said nothing at all. She couldn't.

She was so proud of him. She was so in love with him.

He was giving her another chance.

'You can always change it if you don't like it,' Stefanos said, anxious again. 'If you fancy emeralds, or something modern? When Zoe marries she'll inherit it anyway so it'd be good to have a backup. Anything you like, my darling, just say the word. I believe the only thing non-negotiable in this whole deal is who you get to marry.' And he dropped to one knee. 'If it's okay, that is. If you say yes. Elsa, will you marry me?'

She looked up from the ring. He was kneeling before her. Her prince.

'You're proposing in boxer shorts?' Elsa managed.

'I believe I was wearing a suit and tie last time I proposed. Look where that got me. Now I'm trying a different tack.'

'Zoe, if you run and get my camera, I wouldn't mind this moment being documented,' Elsa murmured—weakly—and Stefanos grinned but he didn't shift from where he was kneeling.

Zoe stared at them both as if they were crazy. 'He's asking you to marry him?'

'I believe…I believe he is. I…can you get the camera?'

'Yes,' she yelled and whooped in excitement and headed for the stairs. 'I want to be a bridesmaid,' she called over her shoulder, and continued whooping all the way up the stairs.

'So now,' Stefanos said, starting to look long-suffering. 'Elsa… My love…' But then he had to pause as the butler's long face appeared around the door.

'Good morning, sir,' he said. 'Happy Christmas. Welcome home. Will you be wanting breakfast?'

'Josef,' Stefanos said, in a goaded voice.

'Yes, sir?'

'You're a servant to the royal family, right?'

'Yes, sir,' Josef said, taking in the tableau in front of him and grinning.

'Then you no doubt know about summary beheadings, boiling in oil and the rest.'

'I have read my history.'

'Excellent,' Stefanos said. 'Then I command you to close that door and lean against it and let no one else in, for fear of blood-curdling retribution, for the next ten minutes. At least.'

'Yes, sir,' Josef said, and chuckled and closed the doors.

'Servants,' Stefanos said. 'You can't do anything with them these days. Now, where were we?'

'Exactly where we were two minutes ago, I believe,' she said cautiously. 'You want me to come down on the floor with you?'

'I want you to hush,' he said. 'Elsa.'

'Stefanos.'

'Will you marry me?' he said again, and again the laughter was gone. Only love remained. Only the gravity of a promise to be made for ever.

And what was a girl to say to that? Well, the obvious one for a start.

'Yes.'

He blinked. 'Pardon?'

'Yes.'

'I haven't used all of my very cogent arguments yet.'

'I'm marrying you anyway.'

'And...why would that be?'

'I believe I love you. Are you sure I can't come down there with you?'

'If you must,' he said and tugged her down so they were kneeling face to face under the Christmas tree. 'Elsa, I love you with all my heart.'

'That's exceedingly fortunate because I love you too.'

'Really?'

'Absolutely. Of course I love you more in tassels and with your dress sword and boots, but I'm so far gone I'll even love you in boxer shorts. Are you going to kiss me yet?'

'You don't want to know how much I love you?'

'You can start telling me,' she said, and smiled as an imperious little voice sounded from the other side of the door.

'They want me in there. I've got the camera. They really, truly want me.'

'Well, I guess you can't tell me how much you love me anyway,' she said, smiling and smiling, and maybe even crying a little as well as he tugged her into his arms and held her close. 'Because I don't think we'll know how much we love each other until the end of eternity.'

'Starting now,' Stefanos said. He sighed and called out, 'Okay, let her in, Josef. Let 'em all in. Bring on the world. The Prince and his affianced wife are ready to receive visitors.'

But not quite. As Josef swung the doors wide they were too busy to receive anyone. For Mrs Elsa Murdoch alias Dr Elsa Langham had changed direction yet again.

The future Princess Elsa of Khryseis was kissing her beloved prince as she intended kissing him for the rest of her life.

'Oh, yuck,' Zoe said in deep disapproval as she was finally admitted. She waited and waited and finally looked around for something to distract her. 'And why is Stefanos's stocking empty?' she demanded of Josef. 'Did Santa forget him?'

'I believe His Highness has his Christmas gift,' the butler told her, and smiled at the pair of them. 'I believe His Royal Highness has his family.'

The christening of Christos Mathew Romanos Antoniadis was an occasion of great joy for the island of Khryseis. The celebration was huge, made more so because it coincided with the opening of the Diamond Isles Medical Base, to be celebrated the next day.

The world had come to see, to celebrate this wondrous occasion and to welcome these three islands into the twenty-first century.

For the difference in these islands in the eighteen months since the old King had died and the new generation of royalty had taken power was nigh on unbelievable. Already the island-ers were prospering, the glittering Diamond Isles finally suc-ceeding in becoming the magical place to live that they'd always promised.

This medical centre was the icing on the cake—a symbol

of all they hoped to achieve. The staff it was attracting had caused its reputation to go before it, and already there were mainlanders waiting to use it. Already the islanders knew that the network of medical centres could cope with their every need. What was more, the medical centre was only the start of the new order. On every island there was employment, optimism and joy.

And now, on this day, that joy was exemplified by the royal family of Khryseis, and this, the christening of their new little son.

Father Antonio performed the ceremony, and the shaky old priest who'd loved the islanders for all his life blessed this baby with all the love in his heart.

Afterwards Elsa stood on the magnificent lawns of the palace grounds, with her husband by her side, with her baby in her arms and she thought the joy she was feeling right now could never be surpassed.

Only of course it could.

Joy is to come...

Stefanos was standing with his arm round her waist, greeting dignitary after dignitary, accepting their congratulations, smiling with a pride as deep as it was joyful.

There it was again. That word... Joy.

Zoe wasn't with them. She and Pip had slipped away, up to the palace balcony to play with Buster and Spike. Elsa glanced up and saw them, two little girls with two cats, a Zoe who was so confident with her new family that clinging was a thing of the past.

Joy.

'Happy, my love?' Stefanos asked as the line of dignitaries finally came to an end.

'How can you doubt it?'

'So...' he smiled into her eyes '...where do we go from here?'

She smiled back at her beloved husband, and she smiled again at her sleeping son. 'Where, indeed?'

'Another baby?'

'Absolutely,' she whispered, gazing down at the perfection of her little son.

'More turtles?'

'Oh, yes.'

'Another cat or two?'

'Two's enough. I'm thinking of a puppy.'

'Is there room for a puppy with two cats?' Stefanos asked, startled, and she grinned.

'I think there's room for anything in our family,' she said. 'This is the Diamond Isles. Place of miracles. Place of wonder. Home of our hearts, and room for all.'

* * * * *

This season we bring you Christmas Treats

*For an early Christmas present Marion Lennox
would like to share a little treat with you...
Happy Christmas to My Readers, from Marion Lennox*

An Australian Christmas is often a lovely mixture of traditional and cool. Our extended family is large, we eat outside at our beach shack, we continue to serve the traditional turkey and pudding, but in deference to the heat we add a few things. Like lobster and prawns to start—and Amy's Christmas Cake after pudding. The 'Cake' is huge—it goes back and forth from the freezer well after Christmas; a lovely, lingering treat for all.

Make it and enjoy, whatever side of the equator you come from. It's a tradition we're willing to share.

Amy's Christmas Cake

For each layer:

> 500 g (or 1 lb) berries (any variety except strawberries)
>   blended and sieved*.
> 4 eggs
> ¾ cup (6 oz or 175g) castor/superfine sugar
> 1 cup (250 ml or ½ pint) whipped cream

1. Cream yolks and sugar.
2. Whisk whites until stiff.
3. Fold in yolk and sugar mixture, and berry mixture.
4. Pour into ice cream maker. Churn until frozen.
5. Pour into large cake-shaped container to form one layer
   of the cake. Cover with plastic food wrap. Freeze.
6. Two days later do another layer with different berries.
   Continue until you run out of bowl, berries or freezer space.

To serve:

Blend and sieve another 250g (½ lb) berries. Sweeten to taste
to make a coulis. (I make this at room temperature and the
sugar dissolves. If your room temperature is not Australian
Christmas room temperature (ie warm), you might need to heat
gently and then cool again before serving.)

Turn cake out. Decorate with extra berries.

Slice and serve, pouring a little of the coulis over the top of
each slice. Enjoy.

*Note from author: Last Christmas I decided to make
deeper layers, and overloaded an ancient food processor
with deep crimson brambleberries. This resulted in a star-
tling non-traditional décor for my kitchen that I advise
you not to try at home.☺

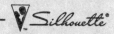

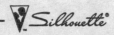
Silhouette

SPECIAL EDITION

**FROM *NEW YORK TIMES* AND *USA TODAY*
BESTSELLING AUTHOR**

KATHLEEN EAGLE

ONE COWBOY,
One Christmas

When bull rider Zach Beaudry appeared
out of thin air on Ann Drexler's ranch,
she thought she was seeing a ghost of
Christmas past. And though Zach had
no memory of their night of passion years
ago, they were about to share a future
he would never forget.

*Available December 2009
wherever books are sold.*

SSE65493

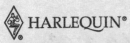

HARLEQUIN®

A Cowboy Christmas
MARIN THOMAS

2 stories in 1!

The holidays are a rough time for widower
Logan Taylor and single dad Fletcher McFadden—
neither hunky cowboy has been lucky in love.
But Christmas is the season of miracles! Logan
meets his match in "A Christmas Baby," while
Fletcher gets a second chance at love in "Marry
Me, Cowboy." This year both cowboys are on
Santa's Nice list!

Available December
wherever books are sold.

"LOVE, HOME & HAPPINESS"

www.eHarlequin.com

HAR75292

HARLEQUIN *Romance*

Coming Next Month

Available December 8, 2009

Whether you want to surround yourself with baubles and bells
or dream of escaping to a warmer climate,
you can with Harlequin® Romance this Christmas.

#4135 AUSTRALIAN BACHELORS, SASSY BRIDES
Margaret Way and Jennie Adams
Two billionaire businessmen, used to calling the shots, are about to
meet their match in the burning heart of Australia. Watch the sparks fly
in these two stories in one exciting volume.

#4136 HER DESERT DREAM Liz Fielding
Trading Places
After trading places with Lady Rose, look-alike Lydia is leaving her job
at the local supermarket behind and jetting off to Sheikh Kalil's desert
kingdom!

#4137 SNOWBOUND BRIDE-TO-BE Cara Colter
Innkeeper Emma is about to discover that the one thing not on her
Christmas list—a heart-stoppingly handsome man with a baby in tow—
is right on her doorstep!

#4138 AND THE BRIDE WORE RED Lucy Gordon
Escape Around the World
Olivia Daley believes the best cure for a broken heart is a radical
change of scenery. Exotic, vibrant China is far enough from rainy, gray
England to be just that!

#4139 THEIR CHRISTMAS FAMILY MIRACLE Caroline Anderson
Finding herself homeless for the holidays, single mom Amelia's
Christmas wish is granted when she's offered an empty picture-perfect
country house to stay in. Then owner Jake steps through the door...

#4140 CONFIDENTIAL: EXPECTING! Jackie Braun
Baby on Board
Journalist Mallory must expose the secrets of elusive radio talk-show
host Logan. As their relationship goes off the record, Mallory is stunned
to discover she's carrying her own little secret....

HRCNMBPA1109